"Oh, my God! Paula, come quick!"

A picture had fallen to the floor. It was not as big as some of the others in the room, but the gilt frame must have been very heavy. It was leaning, tilted sideways, against the brass fender, and underneath it, protruding onto the carpet, was a pair of legs clothed in dark grey trousers and tartan slippers.

"It's killed him!" Jill ran forward. "His best self-portrait. He always said it was his masterpiece . . ."

Books by Anna Clarke
from The Berkley Publishing Group

THE CASE OF THE LUDICROUS LETTERS

ANNA CLARKE

BERKLEY BOOKS, NEW YORK

THE CASE OF THE LUDICROUS LETTERS

A Berkley Book / published by arrangement with the author

PRINTING HISTORY
Berkley edition / January 1994

ISBN: 0-425-14048-2

BERKLEY®
Berkley Books are published by
The Berkley Publishing Group, 200 Madison Avenue, New York, New York 10016.
BERKLEY and the "B" design are trademarks belonging to Berkley Publishing Corporation.

PRINTED IN THE UNITED STATES OF AMERICA

10 9 8 7 6 5 4 3 2 1

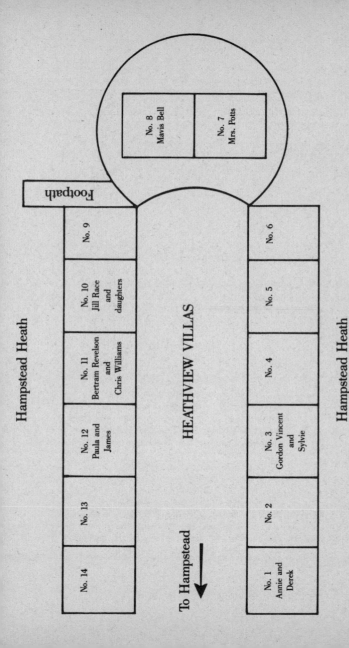

1

"It's women like you who are destroying society."

Paula Glenning, professor of English Literature at the University of London, blinked, took a drink of coffee, and read the words again.

They were printed on plain white paper, size A4, and the two pages of the letter, neatly spaced, looked as if they could have been the product of Paula's own word processor. The long white envelope in which the letter had arrived in the morning's mail was correctly addressed to No. 12, Heathview Villas, Hampstead, London NW.

"Not content with living your own immoral life," read Paula, "you have to go prying into the lives of our great poets and novelists with your mean prurient mind, and . . ."

Quickly, Paula read to the end of the second paragraph. The letter became more and more personally abusive but never actually obscene. In a way she almost wished that it had. Horrible though it was to receive an anonymous letter from some sort of maniac, it was more understandable and therefore less deeply disturbing than to receive a letter that showed evidence of a certain degree of reasoning and self-control.

Somebody really hates me, thought Paula, feeling shaken and sickened; somebody who knows me well. Very well.

For only her closest friends and associates would know her present address. After years of resisting James's suggestion that they should sell their respective apartments in the neighbourhood and buy a larger property together, Paula had casually remarked, only a few weeks ago, "There's one of the Heathview Villas for sale," and James had said, "Let's go and look at it," and they had raced ahead with the purchase, astonished at their own enthusiasm.

Heathview Villas was a small enclave of big rambling late-Victorian houses, a tiny cul-de-sac surrounded on three sides by the rough grass and trees of Hampstead Heath. Several notable literary persons had lived there in the last century, and its present residents included a ninety-year-old artist (male, and retired), and another nonagenarian, a woman who had been writing mystery stories for the past forty years and was still producing them, though at less frequent intervals.

There was also a journalist couple, living together with the assorted offspring of various former marriages; a house full of students of many races; a house with a very exquisite garden where lived a rich old lady and her young male companion; and several houses inhabited by retired couples or single parents. One of the last named, a university colleague of Paula's, had provided her with all the local information, and they had smiled together at the fact that Heathview Villas contained not one single example of what was still regarded in some quarters as a "typical family unit."

"You are evil, your writings are evil," read Paula, "and you will be punished for it. You are to be stoned, your place in hell will be in the fiery lake of burning sulphur."

"Sounds like something from the *Book of Revelations* in *The Bible*," said Paula to herself, "but I'm sure it's not an actual quote."

It was a comfort to be exercising her habit of looking for literary references, and the thought that the letter had been written by some sort of religious maniac somehow made it less scary, more the outcome of generalised malice and less that of spite towards herself.

Nevertheless she felt she had had enough of it for the time being, and she put aside the second page of A4 paper, and tried to concentrate on the rest of her mail, most of which had been forwarded from her old apartment. This contained the usual mixture of junk and notices of meetings, together with a few belated "Welcome to Your New Home" cards. She propped these up on the mantelpiece for James to see when he got back tomorrow, and took up the items that were relevant to the day ahead.

It was no use. Before five minutes had passed she had picked up the anonymous letter again, read another couple of sentences, grimaced with revulsion, put it down and walked across the vast ground-floor room to the long window that opened onto the garden at the back of the house.

Here was comfort indeed, a long rectangle of bright green grass, now partly covered by leaves from the surrounding shrubs and horse-chestnut trees. James knew nothing about gardens at all, and Paula's knowledge was confined to childhood memories of the market garden owned by the grandparents who had reared her, but she and James were going to learn all they could, and they had great plans for the garden.

Peaches, she thought, on the sunny wall at the far end; and apple trees, and masses and masses of roses.

For a few moments her mind was fully occupied with enticing visions and the prospect of many hours of happy activity.

Then the letter took over again. It would not be ignored, and Paula knew that it was going to eat away at her until she could talk to somebody about it and regain her own life-giving sense of self.

If only James hadn't had to go to Scotland for his cousin's funeral. He would be back tomorrow afternoon, but it was now, at this moment, that Paula felt in need of help. Her sister Stella was away too, and Paula's brother-in-law was looking after the children. There was no help to be had there. Donald might even tend to agree with the writer of the letter. In recent years Paula had become quite well-known, outside university circles as well as within, for her lively and well-researched studies of minor literary figures, but she had very little ambition or self-importance in her nature, and it had taken a long time to realise that her success could awaken feelings of envy in some quarters.

The garden ceased to bring comfort, and Paula returned to her chair by the fireplace and poured out some more coffee and picked up the letter once more.

The second page contained accounts of the torments of hell to which evildoers like Paula would be committed, and she found these more ludicrous than frightening. But in the last paragraph the author returned to personal abuse, and concluded, "You are not wanted here. You will find no peace in your new home, nothing but grief and loss and danger. If you value your ill-gotten gains, then go away before it is too late. I remain, in spite of all, your Well-Wisher."

The phone rang as Paula read the last words. It was Jill Race, her colleague who lived two doors away, suggesting that they should share transport to college that morning to save petrol and parking space.

They fixed a time, agreed on Jill's car for today, and Paula's for tomorrow.

Jill was rather older than Paula, a large determined-looking woman who had the air of having struggled much, and expecting more struggles to come. Her two teenage daughters resembled her, and as far as Paula knew, they were much occupied with their life at school and with their own affairs.

"It's a relief to know they've got their own lives," said Jill as she eased her bulk into the tiny Fiat.

"You don't worry about them now, then?"

What an inane remark, thought Paula even as she was speaking; but she was still very shaken by the anonymous letter, following so close upon the upheaval in her life caused by giving up her tiny flat, her haven for so many years.

"Worry," repeated Jill, "could one exist without it? Damn, there's another traffic diversion."

They sat for a long time in a seemingly endless line of cars, trying to find a way into central London. College affairs lasted them for conversation for a few minutes, and then Jill inevitably wondered how Paula was getting on in Heathview Villas and asked if there was anything she could do to help with settling in.

Paula thanked her, said that she and James were slowly unpacking their belongings, and then added, without having intended to do so, "Jill, have you ever had an anonymous letter? I had the most extraordinary missive this morning."

She spoke lightly, trying to make a joke of it to fit in with the sort of superficial relationship she had had with Jill Race up until now.

But Jill did not smile. As the traffic moved on, at last she said, "I'm very sorry about the letter, Paula, but glad you told me. We've never had anything like that in the Villas before, but only yesterday evening Bertie Revelson—"

"The artist?"

"Yes. My neighbour. And yours. He told me he'd had something similar. He didn't show me, but it had obviously shaken him badly. I wanted him to take it to the police but of course he wouldn't and you can't blame him. Why should he have his whole life raked over at his age?"

"It will happen when he dies," said Paula. "After all, he's been famous in his day."

"Yes, but he won't be here to suffer."

For a little while they were silent. Then Jill said, "Will you go to the police, Paula?"

"I don't know. I don't really want to."

"Was it—very offensive?"

"Partly just silly. My living-in-sin without getting married. But also really nasty when it came to my books. And then it shot off into religious mania. A most unbalanced effort. I'm referring to style and content. I wouldn't even have given it a gamma minus."

Again Paula's attempt to strike a lighter note met with little response.

"Bertie's seems to have been the same," said Jill. "I had the feeling he was more upset by the comments on his paintings than by those on his personal life."

"Did he have any idea at all who might have sent it?" asked Paula.

"He said he didn't." Jill manoeuvred the tiny car into the last remaining space in the staff parking lot at the Princess Elizabeth College. "I'm not sure that he was speaking the truth, though. Maybe he would be more forthcoming with a fellow victim. Would you like me to introduce you to him?"

Paula hesitated. She and James had indeed hoped to meet the other residents of Heathview Villas in due course, but in happier circumstances.

"It sounds rather embarrassing," she said at last. "Bertram Revelson, Royal Academy portrait painter, meet Paula Glenning, professor of English and biographer. You have so much in common. You've both received poison-pen letters."

"I don't think he'd see it like that," said Jill. "I think he'd be pleased. And I think it might help you too. When does James get back?"

"Tomorrow afternoon."

"And you're at home this evening?"

"Yes."

"Then we'll fix it. Would you like a lift home? Six o'clock?"

Paula thanked her. One part of herself was already regretting that she had slipped so suddenly into what was bound to be a much more intimate friendship with Jill Race, but such feelings were at this moment outweighed by a sense of relief. Jill was bossy and not particularly stimulating company, but she was well-meaning and reliable and above all she was not the sort of person who would ever write poison-pen letters.

Surely she wasn't. Surely there could not be the faintest suspicion of her being the author?

Or could there be?

2

At eight o'clock they were pushing open the garden gate of No. 11 Heathview Villas. A streetlamp nearby lit up the little patch of grass and the wide stone steps, but there was no light in the porch nor any visible through the stained glass of the front door.

"I believe Chris is away today," said Jill as they approached. "Bertie will be glad of some company."

"Chris?"

"Companion-help," explained Jill. "He's about twenty years younger and has been with Bertie for ages. He must have had a summons from his sister who lives in Brighton, but he'll be back later. He wouldn't leave Bertie alone for long without arranging for a substitute."

She reached out to ring the bell. It was the original Victorian bellpull, restored and polished, and Paula would have remarked on it with interest had she not been feeling increasingly apprehensive about this visit.

"I phoned to say that we were coming," said Jill, "but there was no reply. Bertie can't have had his hearing aid switched on."

She tugged at the bellpull. The sound was startlingly loud, even out here on the porch.

"He ought to hear that," said Jill, "even without his aid."

"Don't you think," began Paula tentatively, and then

stopped. It was no use protesting. Jill had obviously made up her mind to this visit. Whether it was to help Paula or to help the old man or to satisfy her own inquisitiveness, Paula could not tell. She only knew that her companion's detailed knowledge of the lives of her neighbours was rather disturbing, and she could easily imagine Jill Race explaining to some other newcomer that James Goff was gone to visit his relatives in Edinburgh. "He's originally Scottish, you know. Descended from G. E. Goff, the novelist. He and Paula have been lovers for years—everybody knows that. Maybe they'll get married now they've bought this house here. . . ."

And so on and so on.

The clanging of the old bell ceased at last.

"We have to give him time," said Jill. "The poor old chap can only move slowly."

They waited and then Jill rang the bell again and they waited again.

"Perhaps he's gone to bed early," suggested Paula.

"Oh no," said Jill. "It's Thursday. He'll be sitting up late to watch the horror movie."

Paula suppressed a tendency to giggle. I feel as if we're *in* a horror movie, she thought, and she would have said it out loud had it been somebody more on her own wavelength who was standing beside her, and not Jill Race.

"I hope he's all right," said Jill when there was no reaction whatever to the renewed clangour. "I think perhaps we'd better go round to the back door."

Paula agreed. Embarrassment at their intrusion was giving way to genuine concern. She also wanted very much to know what had happened, for although not so blatantly expressed, her own inquisitiveness was in general just as great as that of her companion.

They came down the steps and walked across the grass to the path leading from the tradesmen's entrance to the back door of the house. This had its own porch, less grand than that at the front, and at the side of the door was the usual push-button doorbell.

Jill touched it, at the same time saying, "He's not going to hear this," and tried the doorhandle.

To their surprise the door opened. For the first time since they had set out it was Jill who seemed the more hesitant. Paula could not see her face, but could sense that she was feeling nervous.

"I think we'd better go in," she said firmly. "Don't you, Jill? He might be ill or have had a fall. Do you know where the light switches are?"

They came into what felt like a maze of small utility rooms, all in darkness, and finally emerged into a great, high-ceilinged kitchen, which reminded Paula of a film-set for a Charles Dickens serial. It looked unreal, but was in fact very real, as she discovered when she knocked her leg against a great iron coal-scuttle.

"Surely they don't cook on that range," she muttered to Jill.

"Oh, no. This is their showpiece. There's a nice little kitchen in one of the old sculleries."

"Most extraordinary," said Paula, rubbing her leg.

"Anyway, he's not here," said Jill. "Maybe he's fallen asleep in the drawing-room."

"The other side of the green baize door, I suppose," said Paula rather irritably.

But the period reconstruction did not go to such lengths. They came through a white-painted wooden door into the front hall, which looked rather shabby but no different from that of many other late nineteenth-century dwellings, and both of them turned at once to look at the staircase, saying almost in unison, "At least he hasn't fallen downstairs."

"Maybe he isn't here at all," added Paula. "Couldn't his companion—Chris—have taken him out for the evening?"

"That's impossible." Jill sounded quite shocked. "Bertie Revelson never goes out."

Paula did not feel in a position to dispute this.

"Well, let's look round the house and get it over with," she said impatiently.

She was longing to go home. It was now nearly half-past-eight. There was a television programme she wanted to see; and she had promised to telephone James; and there were letters she ought to write, not to mention getting on with the sorting out of her own books and other personal possessions, many of which still remained in the crates dumped on the floor by the removal men only ten days ago.

Above all, she no longer wished to discuss the poison-pen letter with the old portrait painter, nor with anybody else except James. A normal day's work at college had restored her own balance and dispelled much of the horror and disgust. Provided she didn't actually look at the letter again, its effects could be kept at bay until she and James decided what to do about it.

"This is the drawing-room," said Jill, pushing at a door. "Don't get a shock. It's his home collection."

Paula was glad of the warning. The great room was indeed a picture gallery, a medley of portraits, landscapes and still lifes. All of them, as far as she could judge from her very limited knowledge, had been painted many years ago.

"His own?" she asked Jill.

"Some of them. Others are gifts. Or done by his students. He used to do quite a bit of teaching. It's not exactly a museum of modern art, is it? Personally I find them uninspired."

"All the same, they must be worth a lot. And we just walked into the house!" exclaimed Paula. "No burglar alarms or anything."

"We don't have burglaries here in Heathview Villas," said Jill. "We all keep a watch out for each other. You'll find that several people will have seen us come in— Good Lord! What's happened to the self-portrait?"

Paula followed her towards the fireplace, which was half-hidden by a great high-backed settee, and two equally large armchairs. Immediately above the ornate marble mantelpiece there was a gilt-framed mirror, and to the left of it was a bare stretch of wall.

"The cord's broken," said Jill. "I knew something like this would happen one day. I told Chris—I told Bertie—they're a couple of silly old—oh, my God! Paula, come quick!"

A picture had indeed fallen to the floor. It was not as big as some of the others in the room, but the gilt frame must have been very heavy. It was leaning, tilted sideways, against the brass fender, and underneath it, protruding onto the carpet, was a pair of legs clothed in dark grey trousers and tartan slippers.

"It's killed him!" Jill ran forward. "His best self-portrait. He always said it was his masterpiece."

Paula moved more slowly. Her eyes were on the picture, not on what was underneath. She remembered seeing it in an exhibition many years ago, in the same room as a portrait of James's illustrious novelist grandfather. In fact there had been some similarity between the two faces—thin and hawkish, eyes very pale blue, very cold.

"He's dead," said Jill, looking up from her kneeling position. "He must have been dead some time. He's quite cold."

"Do you know who his doctor is?" asked Paula.

Surprisingly enough, Jill did not, but she knew how to find out. "The phone's in the hall," she said, standing up. "They've never put an extension in here."

While she was gone, Paula dragged herself away from the portrait, which seemed to be hypnotising her, and looked at the place where it had been hanging. It was indeed the cord that had broken. All the rest of the fitting seemed to be intact. She leaned over the picture, not touching it, and saw one piece of broken cord. It was still firmly attached to the frame, but the loose end was very worn and frayed.

Such accidents did happen. Only last year, at her sister Stella's house, Paula's young nephew had had a narrow escape from being hit by a heavy mirror. There had been a great deal of alarm and recrimination, largely directed at Donald, who had been nagged by his wife into doing household-repair jobs for which he was not properly equipped.

This was almost certainly an accident. Perhaps the old artist had been in the habit of frequently straightening the portrait, pulling it about, causing additional damage to an already weakened cord. Or perhaps during cleaning— except that it didn't look as if anything here had been cleaned for a long time. The top of the frame was very dusty, and there was a lot of grime on the wallpaper in the space where the picture had been hanging.

Paula was still staring uneasily at the empty space where it had been hanging, when Jill returned.

"I can't find who his doctor is," she said, "so I've called my own Dr. Garrett. She'll be here very soon."

"We must call the police," said Paula.

"Police! You don't think—"

Jill broke off. Paula's propensity for getting involved in mysterious sudden deaths was well-known among her colleagues.

"There's been a fatal accident," said Paula irritably. "It's a police matter."

It seemed to her that Jill was behaving very naively, quite unlike her usual officious self. Perhaps it was the shock. After all, she had known the old man well, as a friend and neighbour, while to Paula he was only a name in the history of art.

"Yes, of course," said Jill meekly, and left the room again.

Paula continued to stare at the wall where the picture had hung. How could the old man have been standing when it fell?

He couldn't have been standing at all, she decided. However bent and shrunken he might have been, he would still have been too tall for the frame to have hit him as it did. He must have been bending down, leaning over the left-hand end of the brass fender for some reason or other. Only thus, could the falling picture have hit the back of his head.

What could he have been doing? Bending down to pick up something he had dropped? Leaning over because of a sudden attack of breathlessness, or coughing, or pain?

Maybe his heart was weak. He might even have been dead before the picture hit him. In any case, he must have been very troubled in mind if he had recently received just such a poison-pen letter as Paula had received.

She looked down from the wall to the crumpled heap of clothes on the floor and began to feel stirrings of pity and regret. Perhaps they could have comforted each other a little, she and the old man who had also been a victim of somebody's malice. It had been a kindly thought of Jill's, and Paula was beginning to feel rather ashamed of not having responded more graciously.

Where was his anonymous letter now, she wondered, as she looked round the vast museumlike room. Could it possibly be connected with Revelson's death? Victims of hate letters could indeed become very depressed, perhaps even suicidal, but this was certainly no suicide. People didn't pull great weights down onto their heads, nor bend low under them, hoping they would fall.

That was nonsense. All the same, it was odd that the accident should occur now, so soon after the receipt of the letter. Had it perhaps contained a warning?

It was useless to speculate. It was extremely unlikely, thought Paula, that she would ever get a chance to see the letter now.

She turned away, and was walking towards the door when she heard the commotion in the hall. A high voice, not Jill's, was speaking in great agitation. "But what have you done to him? He was perfectly all right when I left."

Jill's voice, equally agitated, seemed to be trying to explain.

"You shouldn't have let him try to straighten the portrait," cried the other voice. "He hasn't got the strength."

"We didn't!" almost shouted Jill. "We've only just got here. We found him dead. He's been dead a long time."

There was a moment of silence before the other voice said: "Dead? He can't be dead. Bertie!"

The door of the drawing-room was pushed open and in came a stocky white-haired man with a plump pink face.

"Bertie!"

He ran towards the fireplace, not noticing Paula, who hurriedly stepped out of his way.

"Bertie!" This time it was a scream.

Jill came up to Paula. "He just won't take it in," she said. "He won't believe he's dead."

They looked at each other in despair, bracing themselves for a hysterical outburst. But the white-haired man—"Chris Williams," whispered Jill to Paula—suddenly became very competent and calm. He knelt down beside the fallen portrait and its victim, then got up again and said quietly, "Yes, you're right. He must have been dead for some time. What have you done?"

"Called a doctor," replied Jill, "and we were just about to call the police."

"Thank you. I'll do it myself. I expect they will want to speak to you, if you don't mind waiting, but you won't want to stay in here. If you'd like to come into the dining-room, Mrs.—?"

Jill supplied Paula's name.

"Professor Glenning." He held open the door for them to go into the somewhat smaller room the other side of the front hall. It was very full of dark mahogany furniture, but around the fireplace was an area that was less forbidding. There were two comfortable-looking leather armchairs, a low table between them, a television set on a trolley, and a drinks-cabinet standing open and obviously much used.

"Help yourselves," said Chris Williams. "I won't be long."

As soon as he had gone, Jill poured whisky for Paula and herself.

"Bertie would have wanted us to," she said. "This is where they mostly live."

"I can see that," said Paula, and then, feeling that she must have sounded too abrupt, she added: "What is Chris really like? I thought at first he was going to break down completely, but now . . ."

"He is very correct," said Jill. "That's Chris. Almost too perfect most of the time, but every now and then he has these screaming fits, always directed at Bertie. I've never seen him away from Bertie. I've no idea what he'd be like on his own, or with other people."

"Did he know about the poison-pen letter?"

"I'm not sure. It was only yesterday evening that Bertie phoned me and said he wanted to show me something, and we sat here having a drink, just as you and I are now, and Chris was in the kitchen making their dinner, and when I'd read the letter I was just about to ask what Chris thought, but at that moment we heard him coming, and Bertie grabbed the letter back and whispered not to talk about it in front of Chris because it would upset him too much."

"So you don't know whether he'd actually seen it?"

"That's right. I didn't stay much longer. Chris is a good cook and doesn't like his meals spoilt by being kept waiting, but Bertie came to the front door with me and I promised to phone him today and fix a time when we could really talk, so when you told me about your letter it seemed to me that it would help you both—oh, hell!" exclaimed Jill, getting up and refilling her glass. "I do feel bad about this. I feel as if it's my fault. And now you've got dragged into it just when you're so busy, but I truly thought that—"

"It's not your fault at all, and you've had a very nasty shock." Paula was thinking as she spoke that she preferred Jill Race being a bossy know-all to Jill Race being tearful and grovelling. "I'm very sorry myself that I never got the chance of meeting him," she added, "quite apart from these wretched letters. And as for me getting involved, well, everybody knows what a disgustingly nosy person I am.

Yes, I'd like some more orange juice, please. I think that's the doctor, or the police. Or both."

The sound of the bell drowned Paula's last words, and they both stood up, drinks in hand, waiting expectantly.

3

Paula stood near the door of the dining-room, listening to the medley of voices coming from the hall, for all the people summoned had indeed arrived together.

Jill had gone to explain to her own doctor that she would not be needed, and Chris's high voice, explaining the situation to Bertram Revelson's doctor, rose above that of the police sergeant trying to get someone to tell him where the accident had taken place. Eventually they all sorted themselves out. Dr. Mary Garrett departed, Dr. George Montague, accompanied by Chris and the two policemen, disappeared into the drawing-room, and a calmer but still very disconsolate Jill rejoined Paula in the dining-room.

"I did explain to Dr. Garrett that we had to call somebody quickly," she said to Paula, "but she's still annoyed about it."

Paula made comforting noises, rather absentmindedly. Her own feelings had undergone a transformation in the last half-hour. The longing to escape and to get on with her own life had almost entirely left her. The unpacking and the letters could wait till another day, and James wouldn't mind how late her phone call was. It was the arrival of Chris that had wrought the change, had brought the sense of living, feeling humanity into this great museum-piece of a dwelling-place, and thoroughly awakened Paula's curiosity about what had happened and what was going to happen next.

Jill was now the one who seemed to be feeling impatient. She poured herself another generous measure of whisky, swallowed it in a gulp and refilled her glass.

"I do wish they'd hurry up and come and take our statements," she said. "The girls will be home any moment now and I never get a chance to talk to them except in the evenings."

Paula continued to soothe, and then, not only because she wanted to take Jill's mind off their present situation, but because she now genuinely wanted to know, she began to ask about the Revelson household.

"Chris orders everything," said Jill. "Bertie is—was—like a child in his hands."

"Not senile?"

"No, the old artist was by no means senile" was Jill's reply. "His mind was as clear as ever, but he did tend to spend a lot of time dreaming over past glories, which was understandable enough, for he had been famous in his day. He had been for some years very frail, and never went beyond the garden gate, but he studied all the art journals and the reviews of current exhibitions, and thoroughly enjoyed himself making virulent comments about the work of young artists.

"Sometimes he would even dictate letters to the artists in question, but Chris didn't always bother to type them, and they certainly never got posted." Jill was quite sure of that.

"What sort of relationship did you have with the all-powerful Chris," Paula asked next.

Jill helped herself from the whisky bottle again before she replied. It seemed that she had never felt at home with Chris, as she always had with Bertie.

"He didn't like me coming," she said. "In fact he didn't like Bertie having any visitors at all. He said it upset Bertie, but that wasn't true. The old boy loved a good gossip. Almost as much as he loved horror movies and chat shows."

"Perhaps Chris was jealous," suggested Paula.

Jill drank, hiccupped, and apologised before she replied. "I don't think Chris was ever jealous," she said at last. "At any rate, not personally jealous. There's never been any sort of personal relationship. I mean, Bertie wasn't gay, and I don't think Chris is either. That's why Bertie was so upset by the letter. His wife died ages ago and he never saw his daughter for years. She married a New Zealander and went to live there. I'm not even sure that she's still alive."

"So who gets his money?" asked Paula bluntly.

Jill didn't know. Bertie never talked about it. One assumed that Chris would inherit the house, and the pictures had probably been left to the nation. But there might be grandchildren, even great-grandchildren. Yes, Jill did know who his lawyer was. He lived in Heathview Villas. Number 3. Gordon Vincent.

"Drives a black Rover," said Jill, whose speech was beginning to show signs of her frequent recourse to the whisky bottle. "And he's got two Alsatians. Takes them out on the Heath. His wife left him last year and he's got a housekeeper, so-called, who is only seventeen. The girls talk to her. I don't."

"Gordon Vincent," said Paula thoughtfully. "I think I've seen him. Tallish, rather sinister-looking guy with dark glasses?"

"That's him. Works in the City."

"I wonder if he's had a poison-pen letter too," said Paula.

It was an idle remark rather than a serious suggestion, made to distract Jill's attention from the drinks-cabinet, and it served its purpose.

"It's funny you should say that," said Jill, leaning back in her chair again. "Melissa—that's my younger one—was talking about him last night and there seems to have been something in the mail a few days ago that put him into a very bad temper."

Paula questioned her further, but that was all Jill knew. Apparently she was not on good terms with Gordon

Vincent. Paula made a mental note to ask James if he knew anything about him. If Gordon Vincent really had received an anonymous letter, that made three of them within a few days.

Maybe all the residents of Heathview Villas were going to receive them. A property developer—trying to get everybody to move out so that he could pull down the houses and build some monstrosity on the site? Or some crazy person among the residents, getting secret satisfaction from watching the results of the letters?

At any rate Paula found it comforting to know that she herself had not been singled out, but more and more she regretted that her talk with Bertram Revelson had never taken place. Was it really pure coincidence that he had had a fatal accident the day after receiving the poison-pen letter? Surely there must be some connection, and Paula, so reluctant at first to be drawn into the old artist's affairs, now knew that she would never rest until she had discovered what it was.

Meanwhile the authorities were carrying out their duties. They were talking in the hall, and the voice of the police sergeant was the loudest.

"Thank you sir," he was saying, presumably to Chris, "but there is no need for you to be present while I take statements from the ladies. They are in here, did you say?"

Chris seemed to be trying to come into the room. The sergeant firmly shut him out and came towards the chairs where Paula and Jill were sitting. He looked very young and slightly ill-at-ease.

"Professor Glenning?" he said.

Paula got up to greet him. Jill stood up too, rather unsteadily, and immediately began to explain that she had been a close friend of the deceased.

Paula could sense her resentment at not being spoken to first, and was grateful to the police sergeant for letting her tell the story.

"So you found the back door open," he stated, glancing at Paula.

"Unlocked," she amended. "Not exactly standing open."

"And the front door? Did you try it?"

Paula glanced at Jill, who was frowning and looking puzzled. "Did we try it?" she muttered. "I can't remember."

"It was shut," said Paula firmly. "One assumed that it was locked."

"But you don't know for sure?"

"It's got a Yale lock," said Jill irritably.

"Yes, madam. Thank you."

The sergeant wrote something in his notebook.

"Did Chris Williams say he left all the doors locked?" asked Jill suddenly. "I bet that's it. He's trying to make out that I'm lying. He's never liked me. I told you, Paula. He's always resented Bertie being friendly with me."

"Yes, you told me," said Paula soothingly, "but I think what's wanted now is evidence." She glanced at the police sergeant, who continued to write, apparently taking no notice of either of them.

But Jill was now unstoppable. "Chris has always hated me, and he didn't really like Bertie either. He was only waiting for him to die. He wanted—he wanted—"

Paula made further attempts to silence her, but without success. It was very evident now that Jill was suffering, not only from shock, but from the effects of rather too much whisky.

At last the sergeant shut his notebook and said, "That's all, I think, ladies. We'll prepare the statements for you to sign and there will of course have to be an inquest. We will keep you informed. Thank you for your co-operation."

Paula, glad of an excuse to get out of the room, accompanied him to the hall, where Chris was standing talking to Dr. Montague. Had they heard Jill's tirade, wondered Paula? It seemed only too likely, but they gave no sign of having done so. Dr. George Montague, small, sixtyish, and unobtrusive, stepped back to shut the door of the drawing-room which had been left wide open, and Chris began a long apology to Paula.

She interrupted his deep regrets that she should have been drawn into the tragedy. "I'm so sorry that I never had the chance to meet Mr. Revelson. I think I had better take Mrs. Race home now. She's had a bad shock and is not very well."

"Naturally she is very upset. Such a close friend."

Without any change in his formal manner, Chris managed to make the words sound very offensive. There was a moment of embarrassed silence. I must get Jill out of here, thought Paula, but she dreaded having to return to the dining-room, and was relieved when Jill appeared, looking flushed and rather dazed but luckily not so talkative.

The police sergeant said something, Dr. Montague held open the front door, and then came the blessed relief of darkness and cool night air.

Jill was now becoming tearful. Paula comforted her as best she could, but kept a firm grip on her arm as they walked the few yards to her own house. There was nobody about, but Paula had the sense of being watched, of curtains in the houses opposite being drawn slightly back, and it was a great relief to reach their destination.

The front door of Jill's house was opened from within before she had finished fumbling in her purse for the key, and a young girl in a skimpy housecoat and obviously having just washed her hair, said: "Hullo, Mum. We've heard about it on the phone from Gordon and Sylvie. I'll make you some coffee."

"She's had a bad shock," said Paula.

"She's drunk," said the girl uncompromisingly.

Paula found herself feeling rather shocked at this remark. She also felt very middle-aged. "You're Carol, aren't you?" she said.

"Right first time. Melissa's in the bathroom. D'you want to come and have some coffee too?"

"Thanks, I will," said Paula, following the now drooping Jill into the house.

One part of her was deeply reluctant to witness the domestic life of the Race household, but the other part of her, now very much in the ascendant, could not resist the chance of learning more about the residents of Heathview Villas. Gordon and Sylvie. Gordon the lawyer in the dark glasses, and Sylvie the so-called housekeeper whom Jill disapproved of as a friend for her daughters. They must indeed be very close to have got together already about the events going on next door.

"You're Professor Glenning, aren't you?" said Carol, propelling her mother before her and glancing over her shoulder at Paula. "Mum's been talking about you. I liked your book about the wives of geniuses."

It was said with the casual approbation of the young, and Paula took it for the compliment that it undoubtedly was.

"Thank you. I'm glad," she said calmly.

Unfortunately Jill had heard this exchange and her fuddled mind had taken some note of it. She began to reproach her daughter for not being more respectful. "Darling . . . Paula's—Paula's a well-known scholar . . . She's—she's—"

"Come on, Ma."

They came into the equivalent of the dining-room next door, and Carol pushed her mother down into a chair.

"Keep an eye on her, will you," she said to Paula. "I won't be long making the coffee."

4

This is obviously the family living-room, thought Paula as she looked around for a chair that hadn't got clothes flung over it or books and newspapers dropped on it.

The contrast with the mahogany dining-room next door could scarcely have been greater. There was a small folding table and a few upright chairs in one corner, but the rest of the room was a jumble of old and new furniture. Paula noticed among many other objects: a guitar propped up on a chair, a vase full of dying chrysanthemums on a low table nearby, and a tray containing a breakfast-cereal packet, sugar, and unwashed crockery.

Often accused of being untidy herself, Paula began to feel some warmth of sympathy for Jill, who appeared now to have fallen asleep in her chair. Where did she do her own work, keep her own books and papers?

Carol, returning with mugs of coffee, answered Paula's unspoken question.

"Mum doesn't usually fall asleep in here. She's got the big room the other side of the hall, but she keeps it locked and Melissa and I haven't got a key."

Good for Jill, thought Paula, but aloud she said: "Thanks, Carol. I needed coffee, but we were only offered alcohol next door. It really was a shock, you know. Finding the old gentleman dead. I'm not surprised it upset your mother."

"Poor old Ma," said Carol carelessly, glancing at Jill. "She'll wake up in a moment. I've seen her much worse than this. When Dad left. That was something!"

She looked back at Paula, seemed to sense disapproval, and paused a moment, obviously not saying what she had been intending to say, but merely remarking that her mother had been a lot better this last year.

At that moment Jill woke up, blinked, looked around, said, "Is that coffee? Thanks, darling," and reached for the mug.

Paula decided that this was the moment to depart, and was just about to say so when there came a ring at the door.

"Melissa's a shit," said Carol, getting up. "She's always in the bath when I need help."

Paula sat down again. If there were to be other callers, then she might as well stay. It looked as if Carol really could be in need of some support. Underneath that bright and brittle manner there was a scared, perhaps an unhappy young creature.

Jill, who seemed to be recovering, began to apologise to Paula.

"It's all right," said Paula. "I'm fine. Carol is looking after me."

"But where is she?"

"Gone to answer the bell."

"But it's too late for visitors," said Jill, sitting upright and passing a hand over her hair. "Do I look very awful?"

"Just a bit weary," replied Paula. "Otherwise all right."

"I'm going to the bathroom." Jill struggled to her feet and hurried out of the room.

Paula, feeling superfluous again, followed her and noticed that she did not go upstairs, but to the back of the house. Presumably the upstairs bathroom was still occupied by the younger daughter.

"Where's Melissa?" said a girl's voice, low and eager, a trifle breathless.

Paula turned to face one of the loveliest young creatures

she had ever seen, black hair alive and shining, as in a shampoo-advertisement, eyes a brilliant blue.

"Upstairs," replied Carol abruptly. "D'you want to go up?"

"Do you mind?" breathed the newcomer. "I *do* want to see her."

Carol gave her a little push in the direction of the staircase, saying, "I'll go and make some more coffee," and disappeared in the direction of the kitchen.

Paula found herself face-to-face with a middle-aged man whom she recognised as Gordon Vincent, the lawyer.

"We'd better introduce ourselves."

They both spoke at once, then stopped, each waiting for the other to continue, and when the silence had lasted too long, they both laughed.

"I'm Paula Glenning," said Paula. "Recently moved into Number Twelve."

"Gordon Vincent, Number Three," said the man, still smiling. "The guy with the black Rover and the two Alsatians and the dark glasses. The black Rover was an exceptional bargain and the Alsatians belonged to my wife and I'm trying to find a home for them, and the dark glasses were worn on the advice of doctors at the Eye Hospital, where I'm having a course of treatment. The trouble has now cleared up, I'm glad to say."

"You look better without them," said Paula, and they both laughed again. Then she added, "I don't know what stories are circulating about me, but maybe I'd better explain that James Goff, a colleague of mine at the University of London, and I have bought the house jointly to see if we can get on with each other on a permanent basis. At the moment we are hopeful."

"I wish you the very best of luck," said Gordon soberly. "As no doubt you already know, my wife has recently left me. Definitely more my fault than hers, although I feel she has more than got her own back on me. Not only have I the dogs to cope with, but also Sylvie. I'd better explain, to complete the record, that that gorgeous girl who has just gone upstairs bears no relationship to me whatever, but is a daughter of my wife's previous husband. Yes, you may well clutch your forehead, Paula. He died recently, bequeathing Sylvie to my wife, who then handed her on to me. A little glamour-puss and two huge dogs. That's revenge, isn't it?"

Paula, looking at him with great interest, smiled her agreement. He had a humourous face, dark, slightly lop-sided, eyes very bright and intelligent behind the untinted spectacles. It was a very long time since she had felt so instantly attracted to any man in this way. Take care, she said to herself. This is the last thing you need, just when you and James are at such a turning point in your lives.

"Surely one of the animal charities can help you with the dogs," she said.

He began to discuss possibilities, instantly taking his cue from her slight change of tone. They moved into the living-room, and when Carol came in with yet more coffee mugs, they had just begun to talk about the events next door.

"Mother says will you excuse her," said Carol to Gordon. "She says she's had enough for tonight and she's gone to bed."

"You look as if you'd like to do the same," said Gordon. "I'm sorry about this intrusion."

"That's okay," said Carol wearily. "Sylvie dragged you along. She and Melissa really are too—"

She yawned widely and did not bother to finish the sentence.

"How am I to get her away?" asked Gordon, looking worried.

"God knows," said Carol. "If you leave her here they'll stay up all night with the stereo full on and Mum and I will get no sleep, and we'll have another of those awful rows and oh, I just can't stand it anymore."

She leaned forward in her chair, her long fair hair falling over her face, and shook her head violently from side to side.

Paula and Gordon exchanged glances, and then Paula got up, signalled to Gordon not to follow her, and made her way upstairs. There was no difficulty in finding where the girls were. As she stepped onto the landing two flights up, she was assailed by a great blast of sound. The door of the room opposite was wide open.

Paula was not tall, and there was nothing formidable in her appearance, but many years of coping with students had given her the ability to exercise authority when she chose to. She walked straight in, identified the source of the blast, pushed at a switch, and turned round to meet the astonished gaze of two young faces. Their expression was almost laughable, eyes wide-open, mouths half-open, gum-chewing temporarily suspended in their surprise.

Melissa was the fair one, Sylvie the dark.

Paula grabbed hold of Sylvie, pulled her up from the bed on which she had been sprawling, and shoved her, only partially resisting, out of the room. They got to the top of the stairs before the protests and the resistance began in earnest.

"Let her go!" screamed Melissa.

"Who are you?" cried Sylvie in a lower key.

"Shut up," said Paula. "I've orders to take you downstairs. And you—" she called over her shoulder to Melissa—"can go downstairs and try to be of some use to your mother and sister instead of behaving like a spoilt selfish little brat."

The howls of protest continued all the way downstairs. At one point Jill appeared in a doorway in a dressing gown, and stared at Paula in alarm.

Paula smiled at her and called out, "Gordon's taking Sylvie home. You'll get some rest soon."

A moment later Carol, apparently recovered, came running upstairs towards them and tried with some success to silence her sister. In the front hall Paula handed Sylvie over to Gordon, who seemed to be trying not to laugh.

"Well done," he said.

"Come on, let's leave them in peace," said Paula, making for the front door.

In the front garden Sylvie's resistance collapsed.

"I don't want to walk with you," she said to Gordon in her little breathless voice. "I want to walk home on my own."

"Suits me. Have you got your key?"

"Yes."

He let her go and she ran away.

"What an evening," said Paula as she and Gordon walked more slowly through Jill's garden gate.

"Yes indeed. Perhaps we could meet again in more normal circumstances. Would you and James care to come round for drinks tomorrow evening? There'll be two or three others there. I can promise you some adult company."

"I'm not sure if James is free," said Paula, "but if so we'd very much like to come."

We're being treated as a couple, James and myself, she was thinking. How different it is, not having our own homes. And suddenly she found herself wishing that she did still have her own home and could accept Gordon's invitation on her own. Alarmed at her thoughts, she added as they paused for a moment at her own front gate after passing Bertie Revelson's house, "Do please tell me how you heard about Mr. Revelson's death. I've been wondering how you could possibly have known."

"Quite simple. Jill Race and I have the same doctor. Mary Garrett. I'd just parked my car when I saw the police car draw up down the road and I stopped a moment wondering what was happening. Then I saw Dr. Garrett come out of the house and along the road to her car which was parked near my place. We don't know each other socially, but in the circumstances a little conversation seemed appropriate, and thus I learned the news. Then I got home and Sylvie told me she wanted to go and see Melissa, but was a little nervous of Melissa's mother, so I suggested she should phone first, and after I'd had something to eat, I'd go along with her. It seemed a good way of satisfying my own curiosity."

"Thank you," said Paula. "All very simple. Does anybody have any secrets at all in Heathview Villas?"

"Plenty," replied Gordon laughing. "We live on several layers. You'll soon find out how to leak the things you don't mind people knowing, and keep to yourself the things you do mind about. Or rather, you choose very carefully the people to whom you tell such things."

These last words were spoken very seriously, and seemed to hold a particular meaning. Paula, with a hand on her own front gate, knew that she ought to say "Goodnight," and go in at once, but found herself questioning him instead.

"Do you mean you don't mind what people say about you and Sylvie, but you choose the people to whom you tell the truth? If it *is* the truth," she added more lightly.

He did not immediately reply, and wishing she had not spoken but unable to stop herself from plunging deeper, Paula went on: "I've a feeling it is true—that she's nothing but a burden to you. But what I'm wondering is why I, on first acquaintance, should instantly be trusted as a confidante."

"I'm wondering that too," he said.

There was a moment's silence, then simultaneously they said, "Goodnight," and parted.

5

The phone was ringing as Paula opened her own front door. She ran towards it and answered rather breathlessly.

"Are you all right?" asked James.

"Yes. Just got in. I was round at Jill's."

Earlier in the evening, which now seemed a long time ago, Paula had intended to tell him about the anonymous letter. And all throughout the business next door, one part of her mind had been relating the drama to James. "You remember the Revelson self-portrait . . ."

Such events had to be shared with James before they felt real.

Then had come the revelations about Jill's drinking and her home-life, which had changed Paula's feelings about her from irritation to sympathy. James knew Jill, and would join in with this change of heart. The phone conversation would have been long, but would have been satisfying to both, and at some point in it, of course, she would have listened to James's news.

But now he was asking her about Jill, and Paula found she didn't want to say anything at all about the evening's events. The reason was only too plain to her. This completely unexpected and rather alarming sudden rapport between Gordon Vincent and herself. It was dwarfing, in her consciousness, everything else that had happened, and on no

33

account must it be mentioned to James. When he was safely home and they were happily settled in their new way of life, then, perhaps, in the right circumstances she might refer to it lightly.

James was asking again if she was all right.

"I'm awfully tired," replied Paula. "There's been such a lot happening. Revelson had a fatal accident next door, and Jill knew him, so we got involved, and . . . Darling, it's a long story. I'm longing to tell you but maybe it had better wait till tomorrow. You must be tired too."

James admitted that he was, and Paula asked about the funeral.

He gave her a short account of it, sounding distant and rather depressed. But why should he be otherwise, Paula said to herself. He was staying in a house of mourning, and although the old lady who had died had been no close relative, James had great family feeling, and the whole event was very much a gathering-of-the-clans.

"They're dropping off one-by-one," he said. "It makes one feel very old."

This was a little call for sympathy to which Paula, putting aside the events of her day and thinking only of the many years of trust and companionship between James and herself, could wholeheartedly respond.

"I've been thinking it would be nice to have a summer-house," she said presently. "At the far end near the copper-beech tree. We could keep the croquet things there. Oh James, do let's make a croquet lawn! I'm sure we've got room. It's such a lovely spiteful game."

The conversation extended itself after all, happily and comfortingly.

"I'll meet you at the airport," said Paula eventually. "What time do you get there?"

He protested, but was obviously very pleased when she insisted that she could make it.

Paula put down the phone feeling much calmer at heart. The house had regained its future. That little glimpse of new horizons that had come to her while she was with Gordon Vincent was already fading, and she must make quite sure that it faded completely, that it became one of those many paths in life that one did not take.

This decision lasted all the time Paula was going round the house, checking that all the doors and windows were locked, but by the time she had finished and was about to get into bed her thoughts had reverted to her anonymous letter, and something of the morning's horrified disgust returned to her. But I'm not the only one, she told herself: There's Bertie Revelson who had one, and maybe Gordon too.

What a pity she had not asked him outright. It would have been easy to do so while they were talking about life in Heathview Villas, about the things that neighbours believed to be true, the real truth behind the rumours.

Layer upon layer. Rumours and truth. All jumbled up. What did one really know of anybody? Whom could one trust?

Paula drifted in and out of sleep. The confused anxieties of dreams blended into waking worries. She could hear strange sounds. She imagined there was somebody in the garden.

She was sleeping one floor up at the back of the house, and beyond the garden was no other building, only Hampstead Heath, civilised by day, a playground for Londoners, but at night a mysterious and dangerous place. Paula, who was rather fond of solitary walks, had promised James that she would not wander down the leafy dells or up the grassy slopes alone after dark. Too many rapes and murders took place there.

Of course if one had a dog, a large fierce dog . . .

An image of two Alsatians came into her mind, together with that of their owner, and she emerged from half-dreaming into full wakefulness.

Why shouldn't she adopt one of Gordon's unwanted Alsatians? James would be delighted. He had been badly missing an animal ever since his cat Rosie had died of old age, shortly before their move. Of course a dog needed more attention, and they were both out all day, but surely they could get over this difficulty.

Paula seriously began to consider the prospect. Such a move would inevitably bring them into closer contact with Gordon, but it would be a normal and happy way for the acquaintance to continue. And James would like Gordon because he wasn't a bore.

Suddenly she sat up in bed and switched on the bedside lamp. That noise could not have been the wind in the trees. It was much more specific. There must be somebody in the garden.

The fence was high, but not impossible to get over. Or one could walk round from the front of the house, as she and Jill had done when they had called on Bertie Revelson next door.

Paula looked at her watch. Only four o'clock, but she was now very wide awake. She might as well get up and do some of the unpacking that she had not done yesterday evening. But first of all she would have a look at the window that opened onto the terrace. That was where the sound seemed to come from.

Ten minutes later she was feeling her way across the huge drawing-room, having decided not to switch on a light. The curtains were undisturbed, and there was no sign of any attempted break-in.

Paula felt weak with relief. She had not realised quite how scared she had been. She unlocked the window and stepped out onto the terrace. The air was autumn-crisp and fresh. The dark outlines of trees showed up clearly against the pink glow of London's night sky. A gust of wind blew fallen leaves about her feet.

For a moment or two Paula stood there taking in the sights and scents and sounds of the very early morning, conscious only of the joy and wonder of being alive, and then she looked around the terrace, her eyes becoming accustomed to the half-light, to see if she could trace the source of the noise she had heard.

It didn't take her long to find the answer. A broken-down old lawn mower which had been left on the grass by the previous owner, had been dragged up onto the flagstones of the terrace and propped up against the side of the window.

Paula was quite sure that was what she had heard, the scraping sound of metal upon stone.

But why? It made no sense. There was no sign of anybody having tried to force the locks or break the glass. Had somebody wanted to attract her attention and lure her out?

The thought was chilling, and she hastily stepped back to the open window. As she did so, she brushed against the handle of the old lawn mower and a piece of white paper fluttered to the ground. It looked as if it had been twisted round the handle, and became partially dislodged by the wind. Her quick movement had finally shifted it.

Paula bent down and picked it up, then retreated into the room and shut and locked the windows. Apprehension had returned in full force. She had been meant to hear the noise and find the paper. The lawn mower had certainly not been moved when she drew the curtains the night before.

She unfolded the paper and read the brief typed message: "It's your turn next."

That was all. Next? After Bertie Revelson? Was she to have a fatal accident?

"Oh, this is too absurd!" Paula exclaimed aloud as she drew the curtains back again and looked out at the night sky. "This sort of thing just doesn't happen."

Except that it had happened next door. An old man had received a poison-pen letter and that old man was now dead.

Pure coincidence. It could be nothing else. Gordon Vincent was very much alive, and it was possible that he too had received such a letter. She would ask him about it this evening. In fact she would talk about it quite openly when she and James went to meet his friends. The sooner the secrecy was broken, the sooner the author of these letters would be uncovered, for surely the malicious and twisted mind of the writer could only work in an atmosphere of secrecy and fear.

Meanwhile she would be very cautious. Absurd though the threat was, she would take it very seriously.

Paula prepared herself a breakfast tray and took it with her to sit by the long window. Mentally she planned her day, up to the time in the mid-afternoon when she was due to meet James at the airport.

First of all she would have a long, lazy bath. Then, at a more reasonable hour, she would phone Jill, enquire how she was, and explain that she was going to drive to college on her own because it would be more convenient. That Jill could be the author of the letters seemed to her now extremely unlikely, but it was not wise to rule anybody out.

Was she safe in her own house? Again, it was extremely unlikely that anybody could have got in and set a booby trap, but she was taking no chances. Keep away from pictures and mirrors. Be very careful opening doors, and on the stairs.

How about the car? That had to remain in the street, for they had no garage. Paula decided to examine it carefully before starting off, and to stop for petrol at the garage five minutes' drive away, where she knew the owner and could invent something that she wanted to have checked for her.

After that she would just have to take her chances with the many thousands enduring the rush-hour traffic. Anybody trying to follow her would have great difficulty in bringing about an accident among such a mob.

And once at college, she would not be alone at all. There was a seminar at nine; she was lecturing at ten, then came a departmental meeting followed by a lunch date with two of her colleagues. It was a busy day, and she could not suspect any of the students and teachers with whom she would be in contact.

The poison-pen letter-writer belonged to the world of

Heathview Villas, Hampstead, and not to that of the Princess Elizabeth College of the University of London. Only Paula herself, and Jill Race, belonged to both worlds.

Nevertheless she was going to be very careful.

Paula put the poison-pen letter and the threatening note into her purse, intending to give them to James to read on the drive back from the airport, and proceeded to carry out her plan for the day.

When she called Jill's number, Carol answered the phone.

"Not to worry," said the girl, interrupting Paula's somewhat embarrassed explanation of why she could not offer a lift to Jill. "Mother isn't well. She's staying in bed today and I'm staying home too."

"I'm so sorry," said Paula. "What about your school?"

"Sixth-form college, if you please," said Carol brightly. "That's all right. They know about my domestic responsibilities."

"I see," said Paula, and felt that she really did see. From Jill she had got the impression that the girls now looked after themselves, leaving their mother free to pursue her own career. Carol's version was very different: Her mother had more or less abdicated responsibility for the household, leaving the elder daughter to cope.

From what Paula had seen for herself, she was more inclined to think that Carol's version was nearer to the truth.

"I'm sorry," she said again. "I hope she'll soon feel better. And if there's anything I can do to help you, Carol, please let me know. Would it be convenient if I called round later this afternoon? About six o'clock?"

"Thanks. I'd be very grateful."

It was said in her most abrupt manner, but Paula felt that it was sincere. That is a brave girl, she said to herself as she prepared to leave the house: I'd like to get to know her better.

She continued to think about Carol Race as she drove to work, but she was not too preoccupied to carry out the precautions that she had planned for her own safety.

— 6 —

James's reaction after reading the anonymous letter and the
threatening note was immediate and specific.

"Take them to the police."

"I know it sounds silly," said Paula, "but I honestly
haven't had time to."

She had, after all, waited until they got home before telling
him the whole story. Cruising along in heavy motorway traffic
was not the best situation in which to discuss the matter. James
was now drinking his favourite China tea and Paula was
refreshing herself with coffee and cigarettes. They were sitting
by the big window that opened onto the terrace, a pleasant
position on this bright October afternoon. They ought to have
been lazily discussing their plans for the garden instead of
worrying about what to do with poison-pen letters. Paula felt
and sympathised with James's annoyance and impatience.
Hand it over to the police, get rid of this unwelcome intrusion
into their new home-life.

If only they could. But it was not so simple. Something
mysterious and unpleasant was going on in Heathview Villas,
and since they were part of the Villas now, they could not
avoid it. We'll get used to it, she thought, James probably more
quickly than herself, for he was by nature more sociable than
she was; and there would be many times when they could

41

enjoy their home together in peace, as indeed they were doing at this moment, in spite of everything.

"It's almost warm enough to sit in the garden," she said lazily. "I do love this time of year."

James seemed to have been following a different train of thought.

"Has Jill Race had a letter?" he asked.

Paula was relieved. This was a sign that James did not intend to try to detach himself from the affairs of the Villas. Usually, in the past, when he had started off resentful of Paula's involvement in other people's affairs, he had ended up by becoming even more absorbed in them than she was.

James, not Paula, was the one who had brought home an abandoned cat and kept her as a pet; and, more recently, had committed himself to paying the boarding-school fees, and generally supervising the education, of an orphaned twelve-year-old girl. I can't resist trying to get to the root of a mystery, thought Paula, looking across at him with great affection, but James actually helps those involved in it, far more than I could ever do.

"I don't know whether Jill's had a letter," she said. "In fact I find I don't know much about Jill at all. Her drink problem, for instance. The fact that the elder girl, Carol, is the mainstay of the household."

James was interested. Paula enlarged on this theme.

"Not the sort of impression Jill likes to give," he said when she had finished. "She wouldn't want anybody to know if she'd had a letter along those lines. Alcoholic and incompetent. That would really hurt. Not like the nonsense in yours."

He picked up Paula's letter and studied it for a while.

"It's odd," he said at last. "There are two distinct elements. All the ludicrous stuff about hellfire, and the other part, the personal malice, bearing some relation to the facts. It's a pity you never saw Revelson's. I was wondering whether the crazy part of it is more or less the same in each one."

"That's a thought. It hadn't occurred to me."

"How can we get hold of another of these letters?"

Paula was just preparing herself to refer, very casually, to Gordon Vincent, when the front doorbell rang.

James swore, but got up to answer it.

He returned half-a-minute later with a tall, fair and very distressed seventeen-year-old girl.

"Carol!" exclaimed Paula, getting up and coming towards her.

"I'm sorry to disturb you," said Carol, "but you were going to come round at six, and you did say—"

She hesitated.

"It's your mother?" asked Paula.

Carol nodded.

"And you'd like me to come round now?"

"Please. If you could. And I'll tell you on the way. It's rather urgent."

"I'll come at once," said Paula. "Won't be long, James."

She turned to speak to him, but he was back at the far end of the room, shutting and locking the windows. "I'm coming too," he said.

As they walked down the garden path towards the front gate, with Carol a few feet ahead, Paula reached for his hand, pressed it, and whispered, "Thanks."

"Another dead body?" he murmured questioningly.

"Oh God, I hope not."

They caught up with Carol, and she began to talk as they walked along together. "Chris Williams is there, terrorising Mother. I can't get rid of him. He's accusing her of stealing Bertie's will."

"His will?" repeated Paula as Carol paused for a moment.

"It's so silly. How could she? His solicitors have got his will, and—"

"Who are his solicitors?" interrupted Paula.

"Gordon's firm. They deal with all Bertie's affairs. Mum knows nothing about it. She never has known."

"Gordon Vincent is the guy with the Alsatians," explained Paula to James. "I haven't yet told you that part of the saga. He was at Jill's yesterday too, and I've just remembered that we've been invited to a drinks-party at his place this evening. Sorry, Carol, please go on."

"That's all really. If you could get rid of Chris for us and calm Mum down."

The girl spoke with a sort of desperate self-control. She's very near breaking point, thought Paula, deliberately slowing her pace as they walked past Revelson's house.

James, slowing down too, turned to Carol. "Where was that will that your mother was accused of taking?"

His matter-of-fact tones seemed to have a steadying effect on her.

"Chris says it was in the bottom drawer of the drinks-cabinet in their dining-room," she replied.

"And when is she accused of taking it?" asked Paula.

"Yesterday. When the police and the doctor were looking at the accident."

"But I was with her all the time. Chris knows that." Paula quickened her step again. "I shall tell him so, Carol. This is just absurd."

The girl began to thank her. Evidently this was what was wanted, and Paula followed Carol into the house determined to deal with the matter as quickly as possible.

"They're in here," said Carol, pushing at the door of the big room, Jill's sanctum, which Paula had not yet seen.

It was sparsely furnished and the curtains and carpet were very shabby. Jill's desk and bookcases were in the far corner to the left of the long window, and that was clearly where she worked, and rested from the turmoil of the house.

She was sitting there now, in a battered old armchair, and sitting opposite her, leaning forward in the desk-chair that had been swung round, was Chris Williams.

Their attitude was more that of conspirators than of tormentor and victim, and Paula glanced at James, sure that he had the same thought—had Carol been telling the truth?

That the girl was worried was obvious enough. She ran across to her mother and put an arm around her neck, and said in a voice that was meant to be comforting but in fact sounded as if it was the speaker who was in need of comfort,

"It's all right, Mum. I've brought Paula. She'll explain that you couldn't have done it."

Chris got to his feet. "Professor Glenning," he said in his most correct manner. "Good afternoon. I didn't expect such an honour."

He turned to James, obviously waiting to be introduced. Paula hurriedly obliged and then plunged straight in.

"Mr. Williams, I understand from Carol that you suspect her mother of having taken Mr. Revelson's will from the bottom drawer of the drinks-cabinet in the dining-room while we were waiting there yesterday for the police to take our statements."

Chris tried to interrupt, but Paula raised her voice and went on: "I can assure you that Mrs. Race did no such thing. For almost the entire time we were in that room together I was sitting opposite her, and when, for a very few seconds, I moved away towards the door, she was still within my line of vision. She most certainly never touched that drawer."

"Professor Glenning," said Chris in a voice that brought the word "unctuous" to Paula's mind, "I cannot possibly doubt the word of a lady of your reputation. In fact, shortly before you arrived, Mrs. Race had herself convinced me that my suspicions of her were unwarranted. There has undoubtedly been a theft, but clearly we shall have to look elsewhere for its perpetrator. And now," he sat down again, "I should like to resume the private conversation that I am having with Mrs. Race."

Paula, quite taken aback, and feeling that she herself had created this anticlimax, looked across at Jill. She was very flushed, and was reaching across to the desk for a half-full tumbler that stood there. Another one stood within Chris's reach, but Paula could see no bottle. She glanced around, wondering where Jill kept her own supply, if indeed she had one, but could see only a low cupboard that might contain anything, and on top of which stood a word processor. Paula's mind immediately went to the poison-pen letters, and then she looked back at Jill and decided the only thing to do was to speak straight out.

"Carol said Mr. Williams was making accusations and threatening you, Jill," she said. "She asked us to come and help. That's why James and I are here. What do you want us to do?"

Jill roused herself. She wasn't drunk, but she certainly sounded nervous.

"Carol takes things too seriously," she said, avoiding her daughter's eye. "Chris and I were having a slight argument but it's all over now and we understand each other perfectly."

"Then you don't need us," said James.

He had put an arm around Carol, who looked as if she was going to launch a physical attack on her mother or on Chris or on both of them.

"I'm very sorry you have been troubled," said Jill coldly. "I assure you that I am perfectly capable of looking after myself."

"No doubt you are right," said James in similar tones, "but since it seems to me that your daughter could do with a little looking after at the moment, Paula and I are taking her home with us for a meal. Where's your sister?" he asked Carol.

"With Sylvie," she muttered.

"Okay. Let's go."

Carol, hand and hair covering her face, accompanied them without another word. When they got home, she asked to use the bathroom and reappeared ten minutes later with hair in place and face repaired. James and Paula were setting out knives and forks on the kitchen table. "It's frozen fish and chips," said Paula. "Won't be long. And there's some chocolate mousse in the freezer. Could you get it out? Thanks, Carol."

"I hope you aren't dieting," said James. "The calorie count is mounting up alarmingly."

By the time they had settled down to eat, Carol was looking a lot more relaxed, but Paula and James refused to talk about her mother until they had finished eating and were drinking coffee, still sitting round the kitchen table.

Paula began: "What's this understanding between your mother and Chris Williams?"

"I don't know. I don't understand it," was the reply. "They've always seemed to dislike each other. Mum said that Chris was jealous of her friendship with Bertie."

"That's what she told me," said Paula. "It sounded quite possible. Has she really changed? Or is she so frightened of him that she is pretending to?"

"I can't understand it at all," said Carol helplessly.

"I was wondering," said James, "just how close your mother really was to the old man. Would there be any suggestion of his leaving her something in his will, for instance? Forgive me for saying that I don't suppose a legacy would be unwelcome."

Carol looked at him gratefully. "We're terribly short of money," she said. "Dad is supposed to pay for Melissa and me, but he's way behind with the payments. Mum can't possibly manage it all on her salary, and we've nothing else. I'm going to get a job as soon as I've done my A-level exams. I wanted to leave school and get one now, but—"

"You mustn't do that," interrupted Paula. "There are ways and means. Has your mother got a good lawyer?"

"She thinks so, but I don't," was the girl's reply. "I want her to switch to Gordon's firm. They really are good. They looked after Bertie. And also Mavis Bell. She writes teenage mystery stories, and she's about a hundred and two, but not the least bit senile."

"Do you read her books?" asked Paula, momentarily diverted from her enquiries into the circumstances of the Race family.

"I used to when I was younger," replied Carol. "They're all the same of course but quite well written."

At that moment the phone rang and James got up to answer it.

"That was the man we've been talking about," he said when he returned a moment or two later. "Your lawyer friend, Carol. We're expected for drinks any time after nine o'clock," he added, turning to Paula. "You did say something about it, love, but we got sidetracked."

Paula, very conscious of her earlier feelings about Gordon, hesitated before responding, but Carol got up from the table at once and said she'd better be getting home.

"Why don't you come with us?" suggested James. "You seem to know the guy well, and I gather your sister is there already."

Paula seconded the suggestion. "Unless you think your mother needs you," she added.

Carol was beginning to look worried again. "I don't trust Chris. I think I'd better go home. I've got an essay to finish."

"We can't argue with that," said James, and he accompanied her to the front door and was gone some time while Paula put the dishes into the dishwasher.

When James returned, he said: "Apparently Jill did have an anonymous letter. Carol has just told me."

"I wonder why she didn't mention it to me before," said Paula.

"A sort of protectiveness, I'd guess. Her mother didn't want anybody to know about it, so Carol kept quiet. She's a very loyal girl, as well as having many other qualities. But now she's beginning to suspect her mother of some sort of—" James paused—"intrigue, I suppose one could call it. I can't think of a better word. Anyway, she felt we ought to know. It came last week. Carol doesn't know what was in it, but she saw Jill open the envelope, read it, looked very sick, and when she asked what it was, Jill said it was some religious maniac, and wouldn't say any more."

"Damn her," said Paula quietly but with feeling. "Letting me tell her about mine and dragging me over to Bertie Revelson to find him dead, instead of telling me about her own letter. Oh well, I don't need to pretend any longer to be friends with Jill Race, but I am concerned about the girl."

"So am I. We'll keep an eye on her. I think we ought to go now. Do we have to dress up?"

"No," said Paula firmly. "It's only our neighbours. Do you realise that we are actually going to meet the residents of Heathview Villas properly for the first time? Are you nervous? I know I am."

7

Paula's nervousness was eased by Gordon's greeting. He was an excellent host, considerate but relaxed, and there was not the slightest suggestion that he and Paula had already progressed in their acquaintanceship.

I have now seen four of the houses here, thought Paula as they were shown into a room where about a dozen people were gathered, and although the buildings are similar, the houses themselves are very different.

Gordon's house appealled to her. After the tasteless muddle of Jill's, and the forbidding museum-piece of Bertram Revelson, she decided that Number 3 Heathview Villas was very much what she would like her own home to be, once she and James had sorted themselves out and carried out some of their plans for improvements.

In the big drawing-room she found herself talking to a tall worried-looking woman of about her own age, whose face seemed vaguely familiar, and a very old lady, small, birdlike and very alert.

"I'm Mavis Bell," said the latter in a surprisingly deep voice. "Welcome to Heathview Villas, Professor Glenning."

She raised her glass. Paula did likewise.

"Thanks." Paula turned to the tall woman. "I've seen you on television," she said.

"Probably," said the other. "Annie the kids' cooking-adviser. I'm not doing it anymore. Too much hassle. Besides, I loathe cooking. I'm really an artist. Mavis and I were discussing the possibility of an illustrated story."

Paula expressed interest and discovered that the project seemed to be more attractive to Annie than it was to Mavis, and the conversation soon changed to book illustrations and art in general, and ended up, naturally and inevitably, in some speculation about the death of Bertram Revelson.

"Paula can tell us more about it," said Mavis. "You actually found him, didn't you?"

Paula felt obliged to give an account of the event. "But I haven't heard any more since then," she concluded. "Does anybody know how the accident happened?"

"Was it an accident? That's what I ask myself," said Annie with a sort of morbid relish.

"Me too," said Mavis. "I asked Rupert about it when he drove me here this evening—he's quite pally with Chris Williams—but he wasn't giving anything away."

"Rupert?" echoed Paula.

"I'm so sorry, my dear," said Mavis. "Mind if I sit down? My legs aren't up to much. I forgot you'd only just come to live here. Rupert is the young man who looks after my neighbour, Mrs. Potts, and myself. She's years younger than I am but she never goes anywhere. We are at the far end of the Villas—that long low house that was built in the nineteen-twenties and that people complain about because it spoils the Victorian ambience. It's divided into two self-contained units, but we made a communicating door so that Rupert could cope with us both."

She paused for breath, and Paula remarked that it sounded a very convenient arrangement.

"Mrs. Potts's solicitors found him for us," continued Mavis. "He was some sort of teacher, I believe, but he has a talent for looking after old ladies, and no doubt he was tempted here by the prospect of inheriting the house plus a great deal of money when she dies. He can have mine too if he likes. I've nobody to leave it to and I don't care what happens to me when I'm dead. They can throw me on the rubbish dump for all I care."

She paused again, this time to take a drink.

Paula, feeling both interested in, and attracted by, the aged novelist, asked further questions.

"Oh no, Rupert doesn't do any cleaning or cooking," said Mavis. "We have an agency that sends us all the household help we require. And a visiting gardener, of course. Rupert looks after the building and runs errands and drives the car."

"And answers the phone and writes letters," put in Annie.

"Only for Mrs. Potts. I have my own secretary."

"Does she or he use a word processor?" asked Paula.

"No, she doesn't," was the uncompromising reply. "She's nearly sixty and she uses a small electric typewriter of the sort that she's used all her working life. She doesn't hold with these new-fangled machines."

"I don't like them either," said Annie, "but Derek wanted one, so we thought we might as well share it. The trouble is that the children want to share it too—both his children and mine."

The conversation about word processors lasted for some time. Paula deliberately kept it going in the hope of getting some clue about the writer of the anonymous letters. Word processors were in use, she discovered, in at least four out of the sixteen houses in Heathview Villas: her own home, Jill's, that of the two free-lance journalists Annie and Derek, and the house in which they were now being entertained— Gordon Vincent's.

There are probably others, thought Paula, and even if some people have no word processor at home, they could have access to one at their place of work or in the houses of friends.

The other two were beginning to look as if their little group had been together for long enough, when Gordon came over with a girl who very much wanted to talk to Mavis, and Annie was temporarily claimed by her Derek, whose face Paula recognised from a television travel series.

"James and I are becoming acquainted," said Gordon to Paula when they were out of earshot. "He tells me you have some reputation among your friends and colleagues as an amateur sleuth."

"Very amateur," said Paula laughing, but with some embarrassment. "I'm dreadfully inquisitive, and several times it's led me into trouble."

"So you will be exercising your talents on the death of Bertie Revelson."

"I've no such intention," said Paula. "I'll probably have to go to the inquest because we actually found him. Jill and I found him together."

"You think it was an accident?"

"It certainly looked like it from what I saw. Why? Is anybody suggesting anything else?"

"My dear Paula, you are certainly not yet wired up to the Heathview Villas information circuit. Of course people are suggesting something else. Chris Williams fixed for the portrait to fall. He's getting tired of the long wait to inherit Bertie's money and decided to hasten the process."

Paula was irritated by the mockery in his voice, but at the same time alarmed to find the initial attraction had not lessened.

"Has he been arrested?" she asked bluntly.

"No. I'm only quoting the rumours."

Gordon's change of tone was noticeable. It was sober and matter-of-fact and contained a suggestion of an apology.

"I suppose there are bound to be rumours," said Paula. "Do you know, I'm beginning to wonder whether James and I made a mistake in buying a house here."

"Oh, don't say that! Please, Paula. I must be giving you the wrong impression about the Villas. There's plenty of gossip, as I told you yesterday, but it doesn't go very deep and it's never malicious. If people want to live really private lives here, they can easily do so."

"How? And who, for example?"

They were standing near to the doorway into the hall,

rather apart from the other groups in the room, but Gordon glanced around before replying in a lowered voice.

"Mrs. Martha Potts, Mavis's neighbour. She's rather arthritic, but she's perfectly capable of getting around if she wants to. She never speaks to anybody in the Villas except Mavis. We know nothing about her except what Mavis chooses to tell us, which is no doubt decided on between them. Come to that, we know very little about Mavis, for all her chatter."

"What about their amanuensis—what was his name?— Rupert."

Paula had not intended to ask this. She had made up her mind to limit her contact with Gordon to the minimum, and certainly never to discuss the other residents of Heathview Villas with him. Was it her natural curiosity that was at fault, or did it lie in Gordon's personality and manner? He was so easy to be with; he invited confidences, he was so sensitive to unspoken shades of feeling.

"Rupert Barstow," said Gordon, "is the most private, and therefore the most mysterious, of us all. He's gone home to check that Mrs. Potts has got everything she needs for the night, but he'll be back shortly and I'll introduce you. Is there anybody else you'd particularly like to meet?"

"Yes," replied Paula, and again she was barely conscious of what she was going to say until the words actually came out, "I should like to meet the author of the anonymous letters."

For the first time since she had first met him, Gordon looked surprised, disturbed, and not fully in command of himself.

"You've had one too," added Paula before he had a chance to speak.

"Yes. Some days ago," he admitted.

"That, to my knowledge, makes four of us in Heathview Villas. You, me, Bertie Revelson and Jill Race. Do you know of any others?"

Paula felt that she sounded unnecessarily aggressive, but

she could find no other way to take advantage of his momentary faltering.

"I'm slightly suspicious about Mavis," he replied, "and I'm almost sure that Annie or Derek has."

"Not both of them? I've been wondering whether one will arrive for James, or whether they pick on only one of a couple."

"I think it's probably only one of a couple, don't you?" said Gordon.

He had recovered himself now, but his manner was not quite as assured as it had been before. We're on equal terms, thought Paula: He's just a little bit scared of me, as I am of him.

"Gordon, who's doing this?" she said in a warmer tone of voice. "What's the object? It really shook me, you know, that letter. A lot of it was just silly, but the rest was really foul."

"Yes, I can imagine."

"Have you done anything about it? The police, for instance?"

He shook his head. "Not much point in it. This is purely a Villas affair. The police will get nowhere. We'll do much better on our own. How about it, Paula? I know the local residents, probably as well as anybody does, and you contribute the unbiased eye of the newcomer, in addition to your instinct for getting at the truth, so together—"

Paula interrupted him. It seemed to be the best way to cope with Gordon. "You're Revelson's lawyer," she said. "What's in his will? And where is it?"

"I'm sorry, but I really ought not to talk about that at the moment."

"Then we're not much of a partnership, are we, if you retreat into professional secrecy when I ask something that I really need to know."

Paula smiled at him as she spoke to show that there was no ill will, put down her glass, and made her way across the room to where James was talking to a middle-aged couple.

They looked pleasant and unthreatening, both the man and the woman, and Paula remembered having seen the man before.

"Didn't we meet yesterday?" she asked.

"We did indeed. For a very brief moment. In less agreeable circumstances."

"Dr. George Montague and Dr. Sheila Montague," said James formally.

Greetings were exchanged, and James added, "The only people here tonight who do not actually live in Heathview Villas."

"Have you come far?" asked Paula, thinking what a relief it was not to be talking to someone with whom one had to be constantly on the defensive, with whom one could not relax for a second into commonplace conversation.

"We're only down the road," replied Dr. Sheila Montague, "a couple of minutes from Hampstead tube station."

"I used to live near there," said Paula, "for—oh, it must have been fifteen years or more."

There followed a discussion about the changes that had taken place in the locality over the past decade. Paula was overcome by a great wave of nostalgia. It's absurd, she said to herself, I'm barely a mile away, and yet I'm in another world. She glanced at James, wondering if he was feeling the same as she was, but for once she was unable to guess his thoughts. The only thing she felt sure about was that he liked the Montagues, as she did herself.

What did he think of Gordon? Could she explain to him, seeking his support, this extraordinary effect that Gordon had on her, and should she tell James about the suggestion that they should try to solve the mystery of the poison-pen letters together?

If Gordon had written them himself, wouldn't that be the sort of thing that would amuse him, to pretend to Paula that he was helping her to solve the mystery?

For a few moments Paula felt absolutely convinced that Gordon was the anonymous letter-writer. She knew it was not herself or James, she didn't want it to be Jill, the two journalists were as yet unknown quantities, and that left Gordon as the only word processor owner in the Villas, as far as she knew. But what could be his motive? Paula could think of nothing except to satisfy his sense of power, his pleasure in manipulating people and watching the results.

"What did you think of Chris Williams?"

James was asking the question. Apparently he had asked it before, but Paula had not heard, being so absorbed in her own train of thought.

"Sorry—I was dreaming," she said. "Chris? Well, he certainly seemed extremely surprised and shocked when he came in and found Mr. Revelson dead. I've no idea whether it was genuine. I'd never met him before. What do you think?"

Her question was addressed to all three listeners, and it was Sheila Montague who replied.

"We don't think that Chris had anything to do with the accident, and he certainly didn't leave the back door of the house unlocked. Bertie must have opened it himself for some reason or another. Of course Chris will inherit something, but that won't compensate him for losing Bertie."

"He really cared for the old man?" said Paula.

"Yes, in his way. George and I—we're in partnership, as you'll have gathered—have attended Bertie Revelson for many years. He was very vain, very self-centred, and not at all easy to get on with. Chris fitted in perfectly. He has no folks of his own—his sister means nothing to him—and his whole life was built on his image of himself as the companion and mainstay of the great artist. That's a fact, isn't it, George?"

"Absolutely," agreed her husband. "Chris loves to dramatise himself, but he's got a great love of routine. I believe he was once an army nurse."

"So you don't think he's capable of violence," said Paula,

glancing at James and thinking of Carol's fear that Chris Williams was "terrorising" her mother.

"Of serious violence, no," replied George. "He likes to play-act sometimes."

"What about scheming?"

"That's very possible," admitted George. "Yes, I think Chris could be quite a schemer. But then we're all schemers at heart."

"I'm not," protested his wife, "and you know it. But I think Paula means something more serious than the usual vague 'if only. . . .' Would Chris write a poison-pen letter, for instance, in the hope of shocking somebody to death?"

"He likes to manipulate people," said George, "but I don't think he'd do anything so drastic. In any case Bertie wasn't shocked to death, nor did he kill himself, nor did anybody else fix that cord so that the portrait fell on his head." Dr. George Montague spoke with conviction. "None of those pictures are properly hung," he went on. "Bertie was a mean old bastard and he got the whole job done on the cheap when he decided not to lend anything for exhibitions anymore."

"He said he decided that," put in Sheila. "Actually he stopped being asked. Revelsons are very much at a discount at the moment. He'll probably come back into fashion again one day, though."

Paula was interested and would have liked to question the Montagues further, but they were interrupted by Annie and Derek, advancing on them with plates of food and bottles of wine, and obviously determined to break up their little circle. The conversation switched to gossip about television personalities until Paula, catching sight of James's barely suppressed yawn, said it was time for them to be going.

8

"I'm glad to get out of that," said James when they had left the house. "Let's walk a bit. I'm longing for some fresh air."

They turned left from Gordon's house, walked past the next two houses, then crossed the road to where a footpath brought them out onto Hampstead Heath. For a while they strolled in silence, then James said: "Funny how different it feels, although we're so near."

"I was thinking just the same," said Paula.

After another short silence, they both spoke at once: "Do you think—?"

They stopped, then James said: "Well, we've done it now. No going back."

"No going back," repeated Paula firmly. "It's going to be all right."

"Provided we don't get too involved with our neighbours," said James.

This was surely the moment to tell him about Gordon's suggestion that they should join forces in detective work. Paula did so. "I almost convinced myself just now that he had written the poison-pen letters," she concluded.

"It's possible, I suppose," said James. "I can't say I liked him. Much too slick. Could be nasty. But I think he'd do things more openly. I can't see that guy being content to enjoy his triumphs in secret. I think we're looking for someone who's not so socially competent, someone more inadequate."

"Jill? But she had a letter too."

"So Carol thinks, and I believed her. But maybe it was something else that gave Jill a shock. An income tax demand or some other huge bill that she couldn't pay. And in any case, Paula, aren't you forgetting that message you found on the terrace?"

"So I am. Nobody else seems to have had one of those."

"Not so far as we know. Actually, that was trespassing," James reminded her. "That is a police matter. What do you think?"

"I'd rather wait a little and see if anything else happens. I was really scared last night, but now that you're home and I know that I'm not being singled out for persecution I feel miles better."

They walked a little in silence along a well-worn path, their eyes becoming accustomed to the darkness, relishing the cool night air and the crispness of the fallen leaves under their feet.

Then Paula said: "We've got to know who is writing these letters and try to get it stopped. Or else—"

"I entirely agree. It'll poison our life here."

They clasped hands and walked on again without speaking for a while.

"Maybe I ought to pretend to go along with Gordon," said Paula presently, "in this partners-in-crime idea. I might learn something."

"It's up to you." There was a slight coolness in the reply. "You know our arrangement."

Paula said nothing, but gripped his hand more tightly. The "arrangement" was a sort of mutual understanding, which for many years hadn't even been put into words, that if either of them seriously wanted to find another partner, then the other would not stand in the way. He must be really upset, thought Paula unhappily, to refer to it now. They had never mentioned it, never even remembered it, as far as she knew, when they took the decision to buy a house together.

Why had she mentioned Gordon's suggestion at all? What a stupid thing to say. If only it could be unsaid! Words of reassurance, of great loyalty and affection, welled up into her mind, but with a great effort she stopped herself from speaking them. James loathed discussions about personal relationships. So did she, as a general rule. Happy relationships, like healthy bodies, were best left alone, not prodded at and analysed.

Paula stood still suddenly, bringing James to a halt with her.

"What's the matter?" he asked.

"I thought I saw a rabbit."

"At this time of night?"

"Well I certainly saw something."

"An owl maybe."

"Owls wouldn't be scuffling in fallen leaves."

"Why not? They've got to catch their prey."

They moved on again, amicably arguing.

"The fact is," said Paula presently, "that neither you nor I know anything about wildlife at all. It's time that was remedied. We've got a big garden now. Lots of nesting places. How about getting a bird-table and really studying them?"

James didn't respond with the enthusiasm that Paula had expected.

"You don't fancy it?" she asked. "Don't fancy the birds?"

"I'm getting old," he said laughing, then added: "But seriously, the fact is that I'm missing Rosie, and cats and birds don't mix."

"You want another cat. Of course. Let's have two. Siamese?"

"No, not Siamese."

"Oh come on, James! Out with it." She shook his arm. "Somebody's got some kittens that need a home."

After some hesitation he admitted that this was true. One of his former neighbours had mentioned it a few days ago in the local pub. Two tabby kittens, one male, one female, house-trained, healthy and hungry.

"Names?" enquired Paula.

"Sally and Sam. Rather silly for cats, I thought," said James. "We could change them."

"I don't see why. Sally and Sam seem fine to me. When shall we fetch them?"

"Tomorrow's Friday. How about Saturday morning? I can give him a call first thing tomorrow."

A little later, when they had turned their steps homewards, James said: "You're quite sure? Cats do take over a house, you know. They get up on your desk and play with your pen and try to stop you writing. Among other things."

"And they get up on your lap and settle down and purr and are very comforting and stress-reducing," said Paula. "Of course I'm sure, you idiot. I can't wait to fetch them. Sally and Sam."

She spoke with great enthusiasm and complete sincerity. Thank heaven for the kittens, she was saying to herself, remembering her crazy notion of taking on one of Gordon's Alsatians. How could she have been so mad?

As they walked back towards Heathview Villas, James began voluntarily to talk of the residents again.

"I'm sorry I didn't get a chance to meet Mavis Bell," he said. "I saw you talking to her. What's she like?"

"Rather formidable. Very shrewd, very down-to-earth. I liked her, best of all the people I've met here so far," added Paula, "and I'm wondering if we could invite her without having everybody else too."

"I don't see why not. We could ask the Montague doctors along. That'd be a nice easy party. Where does Mavis live?"

Paula explained about the divided house at the far end of the Villas. "We ought to be able to get back that way," she added. "I think there's another footpath through to the Heath alongside their garden."

The next few minutes were spent in deciding which path to follow from where they were standing. James plumped for the lower one, Paula thought they needed to go further up the slope before turning, but in her great relief at being at ease with James again, gladly agreed to try his suggestion.

It turned out that his was the wrong choice and they ended by having to scramble up a steep and rather slippery grass slope.

"Sorry," said James rather breathlessly.

"Don't mention it." Paula was rubbing at her ankle. "I don't think it's a *very* bad strain."

She pretended to limp. They were both laughing when they reached the top and could see the outline of the long white house not many yards away.

"There's a gate," said James a little later. "Are you quite sure this is a public footpath."

Paula paused to examine the notice on the low wooden gate. There was a dim streetlamp nearby, and she could just make out the words: NO CYCLISTS, NO HORSES.

"Okay for pedestrians," she called out cheerfully.

The path was very narrow; on either side was a high brick wall.

"I'm never coming this way on my own," said Paula, taking James's arm. "Neither by night nor by day. That must be Mavis's garden. Or Mrs. Potts's. I don't know which of them lives which end. And the other side—what number would that be?"

"The one next to Jill's, I suppose," said James. "Aren't there students there?"

They walked along, very close together, between the high walls, in almost complete darkness. The lamps at either end of the passage shed no light here.

Paula stopped talking suddenly and stood still. She had the feeling that there was another human being not far away. James halted too, and both stiffened, then blinked as a torch flashed in their faces.

"You're out late," said a man's voice.

Paula's first thought was that it was that increasingly rare

phenomenon, a police constable on-the-beat, and seeing that
James was about to retort aggressively, she called out,
"Who's that?" as the torch was switched off.

A man appeared in the dimness before them. They could
make out that he was tall, seemed to be young, was wearing
dark clothes but not a uniform, and spoke with casual
self-confidence.

"We're trying to get back to Heathview Villas," said
Paula. "Can we get through this way? Or do we have to go
round the other end?"

"No problem. This is a public right-of-way," said the
man. "I only wish it weren't. Sorry if I gave you a fright. I
always come along here last thing at night to check if there
are any lurkers. For what use that is. At least it makes the
old girls happier."

"Mavis Bell and Mrs. Potts," said Paula, again forestall-
ing James. "You must be—"

"Rupert Barstow. Pleased to meet you. Professor Glenning and Dr. Goff. Our two new residents. Am I right?"

"You live here?" asked James.

He didn't sound particularly friendly, but at least his
initial resentment seemed to have died down. Paula listened
to Rupert explaining his position in the households of the
two old ladies. It was very much as Mavis had described it.
She had meant to tell James about them on the walk, but had
not got round to it.

"I've no university degree and no professional training,"
she heard Rupert say in reply to a question from James. "I'm
not a bad tennis-player and I can play the trumpet. Add that
to one or two other very minor accomplishments and dump
them into one of those computers that tell you what career
you should follow, and you have—"

"A night-watchman-de-luxe," interrupted James laughing. "Which of them do you play tennis with? Which of
them provides the piano accompaniment to the trumpet?"

Paula was quite taken aback by his change of tone. And
then she said to herself: It's because Rupert obviously

comes from the same sort of social background as James does. How quickly they recognised each other, these former public-school boys from wealthy and privileged homes.

Rupert turned and accompanied them to the end of the footpath and then invited them in for a drink.

Paula hesitated, torn between a desire to learn more about him and the old laides on the one hand, and her own great longing for the day to end on the other.

James had no hesitation in accepting though, and they followed their host through a brightly lit and overheated hallway into a sitting-room that felt small and cosy in comparison with the great reception rooms of the Victorian mansions nearby.

"Make yourselves comfortable," said Rupert after they had all decided that they preferred tea to anything stronger. "I won't be long. And if you don't mind keeping your voices down—she's rather a light sleeper."

After he had left the room Paula said, "Whose house are we in—Mavis's or Mrs. Potts's?"

"I don't know. Let's try and guess," said James.

They got up from their chairs and wandered about the room.

"No photographs, nothing personal at all," said Paula after she had examined the shelf over the fireplace and the top of a sideboard.

"No clues in the pictures either," said James. "Landscapes mostly—they look like originals, but not by anyone famous."

"They've got a very good cleaning agency," said Paula who was now exploring behind the window curtains. "Everything looks spotless."

"No books," muttered James. "Only coffee-table glossies. It's like a dentist's waiting-room. I give up. Have you found anything?"

Paula had given a little squeal of distress. "No, but I've gone and knocked a branch off a cactus on the windowsill," she replied. "Do you think I ought to confess?"

James began to laugh, remembered that they were not supposed to make a noise, and checked himself.

"There. I've planted it alongside," said Paula. "It'll probably grow again. Damn. My fingers are all earthy."

At this moment Rupert came back with a tea tray and halted just inside the door, staring at them. Paula, wiping her fingers on her jacket and feeling embarrassed, moved closer to James, who had picked up a copy of *Vogue* magazine. He put it down, got to his feet, and said cheerfully, "Sorry, Rupert. We haven't gone quite crazy. We were only doing a bit of detective work. You never told us which house we were in, so we thought we'd try to discover for ourselves."

Rupert's face, which had momentarily looked very serious, almost grim, softened into a smile as he put down the tea tray.

"Did you succeed?" he asked lightly.

"No luck," said James. "Not a clue."

"And you?" he turned to Paula.

She shook her head. "But I've damaged a cactus. I'm awfully sorry."

"Pity you didn't finish it off. I loathe the things." Rupert sat down and began to pour the tea. "D'you want to bet on it?"

"Whose house?" said James. "I'll take the mysterious Mrs. Potts. It can't be Mavis. No writer could so completely eliminate all traces of personality."

"And I'll say it is Mavis," said Paula. "From what I saw of her, she keeps her real self to herself. A very private lady."

"Paula's right, Mavis it is," said Rupert, handing her a cup. "She never comes into this room. It's used as a dump for unwanted gifts and for me to entertain my guests."

He spoke very casually, but Paula thought she could detect some underlying resentment. James evidently noticed it too. "Don't you have your own apartment here, then?" he asked.

"No such luck." Rupert seemed glad of the chance to

explain. "I've got a bed-sit with a bathroom in each house, and I usually stay in the other one. Every luxury, every comfort, as they say in the brochures for old people's homes. But no private life."

"Why do you stay then?" asked James bluntly.

"Need you ask?"

"Great expectations?"

"What else? They are both very ancient and very rich. And have no near relations. And I've got expensive tastes."

"You're very honest," put in Paula.

"What's the point of being otherwise? You're newcomers here. If I don't tell you why I do this job, you'll soon learn it from somebody else in this nasty little gossip-shop."

"So you don't like Heathview Villas?"

"In my present position, no, I don't. As a houseowner it's different. You two will fit in fine. I hope you'll be happy here. Let's talk of something else, shall we?"

James asked whether he played any musical instrument other than the trumpet, and that turned into a discussion of brass bands, and thence to jazz, and they discovered that they both had the same tastes, which Paula did not share, and she was almost asleep when James at last suggested that it was time to go.

"We'll fix a time for you to come and hear that recording," said James when they were at the front door.

"Any evening," said Rupert. "I don't have many social engagements."

"Next Monday?"

"It'll be a pleasure."

During the short walk home James said to Paula, "Sorry, love, I could see you were bored."

"It gave me a rest," she said. "I didn't mind. And it was your turn to investigate. But I did find out something."

"Ah! I suspected that cactus from the first."

"It was there all right. And I did knock into it. I got a surprise. I'll tell you why. There are quite big spaces behind those window curtains—like bay windows, but squarer. The one nearest the door was empty, but there was a little table in the other one and on it was—guess what, James."

"A word processor."

"Right first time. Guess what model."

James guessed, and was right yet again.

9

For the next few days James and Paula saw very little of their neighbours in Heathview Villas. The prospect of two lively kittens running about the house was a great spur to finishing unpacking their possessions and finding suitable places for them, and they both worked hard at it until even James was satisfied, and Paula said that she had never been so tidy in all her life.

James was amused. "Cats soon teach their owners not to leave things lying around," he said.

"I expect they'll stay down here with you," retorted Paula. "I'm glad I chose upstairs for my workroom."

She pretended that the kittens would naturally gravitate to James, but actually she was very much looking forward to their arrival, and suspected that she was going to feel very jealous if she didn't get her fair share of them. In the event it was the little female tabby, Sally, who immediately came purring round Paula's ankles, while the bigger one, Sam, attached himself to James.

"Sexist," he said, and tried to make Sam go to Paula, but that was the kittens' first choice, and so it remained.

Much of Sunday was spent playing with them and teaching them to use the cat-door, and a great deal of the remaining time was spent by both humans and animals in dozing in front of a log fire in the big sitting-room.

The front doorbell rang when Paula had got up to make some tea, and reluctantly she turned to answer it.

Carol Race stood there, looking less strained than Paula had yet seen her.

"I've been making jam," she announced. "We had a good crop of plums this year, and I brought you a jar."

She handed it over.

Paula thanked her and invited her to come in. "We'll have some of it for our tea," she said.

If their Sunday peace had to be broken by a visitor, she was thinking, she was glad that it was Carol and not anybody else.

James clearly felt the same. He struggled up out of his armchair, sending an indignant Sam sprawling onto the hearthrug.

"Oh, you've got a cat! Two!" cried Carol ecstatically. "Melissa and I always wanted one but Mother wouldn't have it."

This was the first time Paula had heard Carol mention her sister in a friendly manner, and she decided that the visit had not, this time, arisen out of a family crisis. "How is your mother?" she asked when they were all settled with their tea and cakes, toast and plum jam.

Carol frowned. "She's great pals with Chris Williams. He's apologised for accusing her of stealing Bertie's will. It was in the drawer all the time under some other papers. So he says," she added, removing Sally's paw from the cake she was eating. "I think I preferred it when he and mother were enemies. We'll never get rid of him now. They were still talking about Mrs. Potts's death when I left."

"Mrs. Potts's death?" echoed Paula. "You mean the old lady who shares with Mavis?"

"Oh—didn't you know?" Carol swallowed her cake and allowed Sally to examine her fingers. "She died last night. Rupert found her dead in bed this morning."

Paula and James exchanged glances. "We've been in all

day," said James, "and haven't seen anybody. Was she ill—had she a weak heart perhaps?"

"I don't think so," replied Carol. "At least there wasn't anything serious. Dr. Montague says she swallowed too many sleeping tablets."

"Another death," muttered Paula. "Bertie last week, now Mrs. Potts. Was she in pain or distress?"

"Did she kill herself, you mean," said Carol in her bluntest manner. "I don't know what the doctor thinks. I only know that Chris and Mother are quite sure that Rupert gave her an overdose because he wants her money and is tired of waiting for her to die. They make me sick," she added violently. "Chris in particular. He's supposed to be friends with Rupert and he talks like this behind his back!"

"Hold on a minute," said James. "Don't forget that this is news to Paula and me. Do you know what actually happened?"

"Sorry," said Carol, putting both her plate and the kitten onto the floor. "I was so surprised that you didn't know. Usually everybody in the Villas knows everything within ten minutes of it happening. Chris came in to tell Mother about it around nine o'clock this morning. Melissa wasn't awake and I was making breakfast for Mum and myself in the kitchen."

Carol paused. "This is only Chris's story," she continued after a moment's thought. "I haven't heard anything from anybody else, and Chris is a terrible liar."

"Okay, we understand," said James.

"Well, he says that Rupert phoned him about eight o'clock this morning, very agitated because when he took Mrs. Potts her morning tea tray she seemed to be fast asleep and didn't move when he came in. Normally she is wide awake and says something like, 'Good morning, dear boy, how is the weather?' "

Carol was a good mimic. Paula felt that she had quite a vivid little picture of the daily event.

"She didn't seem to be breathing," Carol went on, "and

there wasn't any pulse. Rupert got in a panic and phoned Chris, who told him he'd be round in fifteen minutes and not to touch anything or do anything until he came."

"Not even call the doctor?" put in James.

"No. Just to wait. Don't forget this is Chris's story," Carol reminded him. "I haven't heard anything from Rupert himself, or from Mavis or Dr. Montague."

"Go on," said James.

"Chris says that when he got there it was plain that Rupert had been comforting himself with the whisky bottle. Chris loves talking about people drinking too much, and he encourages them to, but it's probably true in this case. Anyway, he and Rupert went up together to look at Mrs. Potts and she was lying in exactly the same position and not moving or breathing and Chris told Rupert to go and phone the doctor immediately."

"No phone by the bed?" queried James.

"No. She didn't like to be disturbed. While Rupert was gone, Chris had a good look round and he swears he could smell the whisky on the empty glass on the bedside table. There was a jug of water beside it, half empty, and a tiny porcelain box where she keeps her pills for the night.

"Rupert has to put them out for her. Two to swallow when she went to bed and another one to take if she woke in the night. The bottle was kept in the top drawer of her dressing-table."

"Was Mrs. Potts able to move about the house?" asked Paula.

"Yes, and the garden, and go out if she wanted to," replied Carol. "But she didn't want to, except to visit Mavis once a day."

"So she could have taken whatever drugs or drinks she wanted at anytime," said Paula.

"Of course she could. Chris is deliberately trying to make people think Rupert murdered her."

"But does Rupert know this, and what does Dr. Montague think?" exclaimed Paula.

Carol could not give an answer. "I got so sick of it," she said, "that I just left Chris and Mother talking and decided to do something nice and cheerful like making jam. I'm glad you like it. And I really ought to go now," she added, but Sally had once more settled on her lap, and her claws came out when Carol tried gently to shift her.

"So Chris and your mother are good friends," said James thoughtfully.

"He's mended our fence, which is a great help," admitted Carol, "and told us to call him if we have any trouble with the drains, which we always do when the leaves are falling and block them up, but I wish I knew why he has such a hold over Mother."

"Maybe if you could find your mother's anonymous letter," began Paula.

Carol interrupted. "I think I know where it is. I'm going to get hold of it when I get the chance."

"Have you thought," asked James, "that Chris might have written the letter?"

Carol stared at him as if this was a new idea to her.

"You must have thought of it," he went on. "Paula and I have been going over all the possibilities again and again. We've got to find out somehow. We've invested an awful lot in this house and we don't want our life here darkened by some crazy poison-pen artist."

"Actually I did wonder," began Carol, and then concluded hurriedly, "but it's impossible. I oughtn't even to think such a thing."

James and Paula waited in silence.

"Melissa doesn't want to go to university," said Carol after a little while. "She says she'll get an office job. She's learning typing and word processing at school and she's very angry that Mum won't let her practice at home on her machine."

Paula and James took advantage of this obvious invitation to ask questions, and discovered that Jill Race's locking up of her study was a very sore point with both her daughters.

The older one kept her resentment to herself. The younger one, Melissa, showed it in noisier and more selfish ways when she was at home, and in spending a lot of her time with her friend Sylvie in Gordon Vincent's house.

Further questioning revealed that Melissa was not, in fact, so deeply enamoured of Sylvie as the latter was of her, and much of the attraction of Gordon's house lay in the fact that he possessed a word processor and allowed Melissa to practice on it.

Fifteen-year-old Melissa. Paula's only encounter with her had been as a thoroughly tiresome teenager, but of course there must be a different side to the girl. After Carol had gone she said this to James, and discovered, as was so often the case, that his thoughts had been running along similar lines.

"The odds are that she's got brains," he said. "Whether she's willing to use them is another matter."

"Could she have written the anonymous letters? Carol seems to think it's possible."

"I don't think it's impossible. We've just assumed that they were written by an older person. Let's have another look at yours."

Paula reached out for her handbag. She had not been able to decide where to put the letter and had ended by carrying the wretched thing about with her for safe keeping.

"No, I don't think it could be Melissa," she said after she and James had studied it together. "There's too much of an adult attitude in it. It's more likely to be her mother."

"Jill? I shouldn't have thought she had the imagination. The girl seems to me more likely," said James. "She could be a good mimic, like her sister. We simply don't know."

"I suppose it could be her idea of a joke," admitted Paula. "Or some sort of revenge. Oh, James! I've just thought. Revenge. That threatening note I found on the old lawn mower. That's much more like Melissa. Or Sylvie. Where did I put it?"

"Keep calm," said James, producing the slip of paper

from his wallet. "You gave it to me. You were somewhat agitated when you told me about it."

"IT'S YOUR TURN NEXT."

Paula read the words aloud, recalling her sense of horror and alarm when she had first seen them. But then she had had some unpleasant shocks and a sleepless night. Sitting comfortably by a log fire with James and the little cats on this quiet Sunday afternoon, she felt very differently. The typed message, taken out of context, looked merely rather childish and silly.

"Yes, I think it's quite possible that Melissa put it there," she said. "That would make sense. She was furious with me for forcibly ejecting Sylvie. And so was Sylvie. Either of them could have done it. Or both."

"Typewriters can be identified," said James. "We don't know what machines Sylvie has access to, but Melissa would have had to use the one she has at home. She couldn't, surely, have got hold of any other at that time of night. Anyway, we can easily check this."

"I don't see how," said Paula. "Melissa wouldn't speak to me. And I'm not in her mother's favour, either."

"Then we'll have to ask Carol," said James, putting away the slip of paper. "Let's think of an excuse to go round there. Did she leave anything behind just now?"

"No, but I did promise her some books." Paula got up from her chair. "Are you thinking of going now?"

James was already at the opposite side of the room, scanning the bookshelves. "There's a book that I mentioned to Rupert," he muttered. "We might as well make enquiries all round while we're about it. Of course we'll have to pretend to him that we haven't heard about Mrs. Potts dying. We'll be very surprised at the news."

"He probably won't even mention it," said Paula, "if you start talking jazz again. I don't think I can stand it."

"Then I'll go alone, and you can do Carol and Melissa."

"Which will no doubt mean having to see Jill," said

Paula. "Oh well, I suppose I ought to enquire how she is. What do we do with the cats when we are out, James?"

"Kitchen," he replied firmly, scooping them both up, "until they're old enough to have some respect for the niceties of human existence."

10

"Typewriters," said Paula to herself as she stood on the doorstep of Number 10 Heathview Villas, while James walked on to the end of the roadway on his own errand. "How am I going to think of an excuse to look at all the typewriters in the house?"

After a long wait, the door was opened by Chris Williams.

"Professor Glenning," he said in his blandest manner, "to what do we owe the honour of this visit?"

"I've come to see Carol," said Paula, equally calmly. "I've got some books I promised her."

Chris stepped back to allow her to enter. "You are probably wondering why I came to the door," he said, lowering his voice. "The fact is that our mutual friend, Carol's mother, is—shall we say—not quite herself?"

"Do you mean she's drunk?"

Chris looked shocked. "We don't call it that," he said reproachfully.

Paula almost retorted "Carol does," but restrained herself. Chris Williams had clearly acquired a privileged position in this household and she must keep on good terms with him if she was to get an opportunity to examine the typewriters.

"I won't disturb her if she doesn't want to see anybody," she said, "but I would like to give these books to Carol."

"I'll give them to her." He held out a hand.

"Thank you, but I'd rather see her. There's something I want to explain."

"Please yourself. She went upstairs."

He shrugged and turned into the room on the left, Jill's own workroom, leaving Paula with the certainty that he disliked her or was suspicious of her, or both.

This was not a pleasant feeling. Chris Williams, if he had indeed inherited Bertie Revelson's house and intended to live there, would be her neighbour for the foreseeable future. It was inconceivable that he could work himself into the position of dominating her home and James's as he was now doing with Jill's house, but all the same there were plenty of ways in which a neighbour could make himself disagreeable.

Our garden, thought Paula as she made her way upstairs. He overlooks quite a lot of our garden. And then there are the kittens.

When she arrived at the second landing she heard voices coming from the room out of which she had dragged Sylvie some days ago.

Paula knocked on the door, and after a moment's silence it was opened by Melissa. She looked very different from the furious teenager who had screamed at Paula for ejecting her friend. Shorter than Carol, rather more stockily built, but with the same hair, the same eyes, the same defensive but determined air.

She was about to speak, but Paula got in first.

"I must apologise for the way I behaved to you and Sylvie the other day."

Carol, joining her sister in the doorway, gave Melissa a nudge. "You deserved it, the two of you."

"I know," said Melissa. "I'm sorry. It's teenage tantrums, you know. I'm going through a phase." She pulled a face. "Come in, Paula—may I call you Paula?—we're having a conference, Carol and me. What we are going to do about our mother. Come and help."

She swept a pile of clothes off the end of the bed to make room for Paula to sit down.

"Here's your books, Carol," said Paula. "We'll talk about them some other time." She looked from one to the other of the girls. "What's been happening? Chris Williams told me that your mother was—er—not quite herself." She mimicked his voice. "I'm afraid I upset him by asking outright if she was drunk."

"Chris is a shit," said the younger girl, and her sister concurred.

"But why," asked Paula, "does your mother let him behave like this?"

"We don't know," said the sisters in chorus.

"Except," added Carol, "that we think we may have a clue. Mel and I were discussing it just now. Shall we tell her?"

Melissa nodded. She was biting her lips and glancing uncertainly at Paula. Suddenly she burst out. "But I've got to tell her something else first. Go away, Carol. Go and look in that place you thought of. I don't want you to know about this."

To Paula's surprise, Carol got up at once. "I'll fetch some coffee too," she said, and left the room.

"We're okay now," said Melissa, "Carol and me, because we both hate Chris. But we've had these truces before, and they don't last. That's why I don't want her to know. She'll throw it back at me forever. I wish I'd never done it, anyway."

Paula waited without speaking.

"This is a confession," went on Melissa, "as you've probably guessed. That silly note. You must have found it because I saw you'd moved the old lawn mower by your window."

"Do you mean that threatening note?"

Paula had a hard time restraining herself from laughing aloud at the ease with which her own errand was being accomplished. There was no need to make excuses for looking at typewriters. Melissa was handing her the answer, but she must be very sober about it, even pretend to be angry. If she were to laugh now, or make light of the note, she would make an enemy of the girl forever.

"It scared me silly," Paula said. "I'd had that revolting poison-pen letter the day before, and then finding Mr. Revelson dead, and I'd had hardly any sleep. I got really panicky."

"I'm terribly sorry," said Melissa, and Paula suspected that there was some gratification mixed with her genuine remorse. "I just didn't think. I was so mad with you that evening. We hadn't even been introduced and you came upstairs like—"

"Please, please," broke in Paula. "I've got to apologise too. I never ought to have behaved as I did."

"It worked, though," said Melissa. "As a matter of fact there are times when I want to be rid of Sylvie myself." She began to laugh, and with great relief Paula joined in.

"So nobody else knows about this," she said presently. "Do you mind if I tell James? I promise you neither of us will tell anyone else. Ever."

"Thanks," said Melissa, "but actually I think someone else does know. I mean he doesn't know what I was doing, but he knows I was out in the middle of the night."

"Chris Williams?"

Melissa nodded. "I had to come past his house to get to yours. He was in the front garden, leaning over the gate."

"He spoke to you?"

"He said, 'What are you doing, prowling about at this hour?'—and I said, 'What are you doing yourself?' Then he said something like 'I can't sleep, my life is in ruins'—all melodramatic, you know how he gets sometimes. And I said, 'Yes, I'm sorry about Mr. Revelson,' and came away, but just as I was coming into our front garden I saw somebody coming along the road and I got behind the laurel bushes so that he didn't see me as he came past."

She paused, and Paula gratified her by asking if she saw who it was.

"Rupert Barstow," replied Melissa triumphantly. "The guy who lives with the two old dames. Have you met him?"

"Yes," replied Paula. "We met him during some nocturnal wandering, but it wasn't so late at night. What happened next?"

"He came up to Chris and said something—I couldn't hear, and I couldn't see properly from behind the bush—and in any case the street lighting isn't much use—but I do know that they went into the house together—round to the back door, and I waited a bit but nobody came out. And Paula, I don't know whether you'll think I'm imagining things, but you know old Mrs. Potts was found dead in her bed this morning, and Rupert phoned Chris—"

She paused, and Paula said, "Yes, I had heard something about it. Not any details though."

"We've been talking about it, Carol and me and Mother too, before Chris turned up, and Mother was quite sure that Rupert had done it. But Carol said no, and I don't know what to think. Of course I didn't say anything to the others about seeing them both that night, and please, *please* don't say anything if we talk about it, but I can't help wondering—"

Melissa broke off again.

"You're wondering whether there was some sort of plot, conspiracy, something or other, between Chris and Rupert. Is that it?" asked Paula.

"Yes. Do you think that's very silly?"

"I don't think it's silly at all," said Paula. She thought a moment before she added, "Melissa, I may be imagining things, and I don't want to be an alarmist, but there certainly seems to be something very nasty going on in this neighbourhood. You'll be careful, won't you?"

"You mean somebody might think I know something that I ought not to know," said the girl. "I'd thought of that. I'm certainly not going to wander about in the middle of the night anymore, nor all that much in the daytime either."

"Good girl. I can't imagine that you are in any real danger, but I do think it's wise to be careful."

"I'm glad I've told you." Melissa got up. "Carol's being a long time. I wonder if she has found that letter."

"You mean your mother's—" began Paula.

Melissa put a finger to her lips. The door opened and Carol came in with a tray, placed it precariously on top of the things that covered the dressing-table, and said brightly, "Success! It was in her bedroom."

"Gimme!" cried Melissa, rushing forward.

Carol fended her off. "Wait. I haven't read it myself yet. We'll read it together."

They took their coffee and rearranged themselves on the bed, Carol in the centre, Paula and Melissa either side of her. Two sheets of paper, A4 size, lay on Carol's lap.

"Can you see?" asked Carol.

"Yes," chorused the others.

It's the same layout, thought Paula, and looks like the same print.

"Dear Jill," she read to herself, "what a silly woman you are. Silly Jilly. As if everybody didn't know that you're a fat old boozer. There's a place in the seventh circle of hell for the likes of you."

Paula was sitting very close to Carol and could feel the strain in the girl as she read. She put an arm round her and wished she could hold Melissa too. Poor children, she thought, feeling Jill's shock as well as re-living the shock of her own letter.

"Just a minute," said Carol. She bent down and put her coffee mug on the floor. Her voice was steady but she was very tense. She straightened up again and took hold of Melissa's hand. "Okay. Tell me when you're ready for the next page."

Without any further interruption they all three read through to the end. Paula waited for the girls to speak, and when they didn't she said in a matter-of-fact way, "It's the same mixture as my letter—an awful lot of eternal damnation nonsense with some nasty personal bits in between."

Carol was scarcely listening. "I suppose that's it," she said wretchedly, staring at the letter. "A piddling little tax fiddle. Chris must have found out and threatened to tell the tax office. Oh, it's so silly! Why did she have to do it? We could have saved money in other ways. Taken in lodgers. There's lots of room in this house."

"Yuk," said Melissa, "lodgers."

"Lots of people have to," said her sister.

It looked as if an argument was threatening. Paula hastily intervened. "If your mother really did make false statements to the Inland Revenue," she said, "who could possibly have known about it? Does she have an accountant?"

"No, she does her own tax forms."

There was a silence. Both girls were slumped back on the bed, looking very dejected. Paula wanted to ask some questions, but was hesitant lest it should add to their distress. Then suddenly Melissa said: "Dad would have known about it."

"You're right," said her sister. "He probably put her up to it."

"Your father?" prompted Paula.

"There's no need to be tactful," said Carol in her most aggressive manner. "Everybody knows the story. He drank. Much more than Mother. Too much even for a journalist. He got the sack from his job four years ago and went off to California with a woman much older than himself who's got lots of money. I'm sure she makes him miserable. I hope she does," she added defiantly.

"I don't," said Melissa in a low voice that threatened tears. "I miss him. Still."

"You've got Roger," said her sister.

"And you've got Steve."

"It's not the same."

The girls were huddling together now. Paula looked at

them with helpless pity. But at least, she thought, there seems to be no rivalry over their boy friends. She picked up the poison-pen letter that Carol had let fall and studied it for a moment or two.

"The writer obviously knew about your father," she said. "Could he possibly have written it himself—or the woman he now lives with?"

They thought not. In any case, the letters must surely be the work of one person, and the girls' father could not possibly have written the letter that Paula had received.

"That brings us back to Heathview Villas," she said. "What's your opinion, Melissa?"

"I'm sure it's Chris," was the muttered reply, and then she went on, before Paula had a chance to ask why, "or Rupert."

"Why should it be Rupert?" asked her sister.

"They're thick as thieves."

"No, they're not," said Carol.

But they met in the middle of the night, thought Paula, and I've promised to say nothing about it. "Where could Chris get access to a word processor?" she asked.

"Gordon lets him use his sometimes. So Sylvie says," said Melissa.

"You don't possibly think that Gordon Vincent," began Paula very tentatively.

This produced rather a difference of opinion. Carol thought it unlikely that Gordon would do anything like anonymous letter-writing. He had been helpful to them since their parents' divorce, and he was said to be a very good lawyer.

Melissa was not so sure. "Yes, Gordon had helped a lot, but . . ."

"But what?" asked Carol.

"Well, *you* know what he's like," said Melissa.

"There's a lot of gossip. There always is when a marriage breaks up."

"Yes, I know, but—"

Again Melissa seemed nervous about continuing.

Paula decided to intervene. "What was his wife like?" she asked. "To look at, I mean," she added as neither girl seemed inclined to reply.

"Very glamorous," said Melissa instantly.

"If you like dumb blondes," put in her sister.

Melissa protested, but Paula rather got the impression that the absent Mrs. Vincent had not been her husband's equal in intelligence or education. "You don't think she could have written the letters?" she asked.

The sisters took time to consider this suggestion seriously, Carol with some enthusiasm for the idea, and Melissa, who was plainly pro-Mrs. Vincent, less eagerly. Both agreed, however, that it was not impossible. Gordon's wife had done part-time office work and knew about word processors. And she had also belonged to one of those funny churches—not one of the well-known ones but rather similar—where they didn't believe in evolution. Gordon told funny stories about it. Yes, the more they thought about it, the more the girls thought that she could have been the writer. Certainly she had disliked their mother, Jill.

"But what about me?" asked Paula. "Could she know anything about me?"

"I don't see why not," said Melissa. "She's living in Hampstead. Sylvie goes to visit her."

"And Sylvie would know about me and James. I see," said Paula thoughtfully. "I've had rather a wild idea," she added, getting up because the girls had done so. "Suppose Gordon's wife had written a poison-pen letter to him, out of spite, but didn't want to be identified, so she wrote to other people too as a cover?"

Neither Carol nor Melissa thought much of this idea. "I'm sure she wouldn't do anything like that," said Melissa, "and I'm sure Gordon would know if she'd written the letter he had. I still think it's more likely to be Chris."

Paula dropped the subject. It was very obvious that the two of them wanted to be on their own to discuss their mother's affairs, but they both came with her to the front door.

"By the way," said Paula just before she left, "what is the name of Gordon's wife?"

"Sylvia," replied Melissa. "Goodnight. And thanks for everything."

11

"Who is Sylvia, what is she?" quoted Paula to herself as she stood on the bottom doorstep after saying goodnight to Melissa.

Gordon's wife—or ex-wife, for it didn't seem to matter much nowadays whether people were divorced or not—seemed to Paula to be a very good candidate for the poison-pen letter-writer. "One of those funny religions," would account for all the hellfire business, and if she was regularly seeing her young relative Sylvie, then she would know all the gossip about the residents of Heathview Villas.

Paula was very tempted to cross the road and walk the short distance to Gordon's house and make some excuse for calling at this hour on a Sunday evening, but she finally decided against it. How could she convince him that she was there to carry out her own detective work when she wasn't even sure that this was her only motive? Of course he would assume that she was "making advances" as one used to say, and to start asking questions about his wife would mean a rapid slide into closer intimacy.

The attraction was too strong, and must be resisted. There are the kittens, she thought, smiling to herself as she walked towards the gate. James and I must never break up our household. We've got to adapt ourselves to the life here, and we've got to find that letter-writer.

Without making any conscious decision, Paula turned left after closing Jill's gate and walked towards the long white house at the far end of the road. If James and Rupert were talking jazz again she would just have to put up with it.

Outside Mavis's entrance she hesitated once more. The building really did not fit into this little Victorian enclave. Angular, stark, and undecorated, it was very much a relic of the early part of the twentieth century. Well before my time, thought Paula; and for those two youngsters whom she had just left, it was way back in history. It didn't "feel right," as the Victorian dwellings did; but at the time it must have been somebody's pride and joy. Very modern, very avant-garde. And with a most unobtrusive front entrance at the end of the short driveway. The separate garage, farther to the left, was the only one in the street. That must have been a great status symbol when it was built.

Feeling vaguely saddened by these thoughts about the passage of time, Paula rang the bell. After a longish wait, Rupert came to the door.

"Is James here?" she asked. "He said he was coming."

"Yes, he's here. Sorry I was so long answering the bell. We're sitting in the other house—Mrs. Potts's."

"If I'd known that I'd have gone to the other entrance," said Paula, following him into the hall.

"We hardly ever use it," said Rupert, pushing at a door to his right. "She never goes out and rarely has visitors. We go through her drawing-room. Mind the furniture."

Paula followed him into a completely different atmosphere. Mavis's main reception room had been stark and impersonal. Her neighbor's was oppressively overcrowded. Like a junk shop, thought Paula, and then, pausing to look at a cabinet full of porcelain, she amended her impressions: not junk, more like a museum.

"Staffordshire, isn't it?" she said. "And a real Chippendale chair! No wonder you're worried about security, Rupert. There must be a fortune in this room."

"Fortune is right," he said, looking very worried. "And

she's not even adequately insured. Her solicitors are always going on at me about it. But there's nothing I can do. I've nothing to do with her business affairs. One of the partners comes in once a week, on Monday mornings, to discuss anything that arises, and to give me my instructions if there is anything that concerns me. They pay my salary plus an amount for household expenses. She won't talk money with me at all."

Suddenly he stood still and exclaimed: "I'm talking as if she's still alive. But she's dead."

He looked quite bewildered. He's genuinely shocked, thought Paula, or else he's a superb actor.

"Who are the lawyers," she asked, "who handled everything for Mrs. Potts?"

"Oh—Gordon Vincent's firm. Not Gordon himself. One of his partners. We'll go upstairs now—to my bed-sit, if you don't mind. This room gives me the horrors."

He walked on again, visibly shuddering, and passing dangerously near to what looked like an early Wedgewood vase standing too near the edge of a little inlaid table. Paula, following more carefully, was glad when they reached the further side of the room.

"Why did they make the connecting door come straight into the main reception room?" she asked when they were standing in a comparatively uncrowded hall at the foot of a staircase.

Rupert shrugged. "Search me. I'm not an architect. There's another door linking the two kitchens. I normally use that, but when it's a visitor . . ."

His voice trailed away. He really does seem distracted, thought Paula as she followed him upstairs, but it could well be an act. Maybe he wanted to show me that room and explain that he had nothing to do with her finances. And to mention Gordon. He crops up everywhere.

They reached the top of the staircase.

"That's her bedroom," said Rupert indicating a closed door on the left. "I'm at the back of the house. The servants' quarters. Takes a lot of getting used to, you know, when you're not brought up to it."

He seemed to be talking almost at random. There was no sign of the self-assurance that Paula had noticed at their previous meeting. He's not cool and calculating enough to be a murderer, she thought; surely this is not an act—he's shocked silly, and terrified of being suspected.

She followed him into a fair-sized room, plainly but adequately furnished with a divan bed, a writing desk, bookshelves, and chairs and tables. Two of the chairs were occupied: James got to his feet as they came in, and Mavis looked up at them and apologised for not rising.

"I'm very arthritic today," she said. "It's been a great shock, my neighbour dying. At our age one ought to expect it, but one doesn't."

Paula expressed her sympathy and concern. She does look bad, she added to herself, thinking that Mavis could do with more reliable company than Rupert at this time. Supposing she suspected him, or even knew that he was guilty? Somebody really ought to be looking after her.

"I'm feeling very ancient," went on Mavis, as if reading Paula's thoughts. "And rather nervous. And Rupert is very worried about me. He doesn't want to be responsible for me. Not that he looks after my medicines. I do that myself."

She smiled up at him, but there was much more malevolence than amusement in her tone of voice.

"And if I ever become too senile to know what I'm swallowing," she added, "then I'd rather be dead. Make a note of that, Rupert."

"You'll never be senile," said Rupert, sounding much more like his former self, "not if you live till one-hundred-and-three."

"Probably not," she snapped, "but I'm nervous nevertheless." She turned to Paula and James. "I have angina, among various other tiresome ailments, and I would be happier if I knew there was somebody in my house on whom I could rely in an emergency."

"I told you I'd phone the nursing agency for you," said Rupert.

"Yes, dear boy, I know you did, but you know I can't stand those brisk and bossy creatures who have always wanted to meet a famous author, and treat you as a cross between an idiot child and a rare specimen in the zoo. No. I've made other arrangements."

She paused for somebody to ask what they were, but nobody spoke. It would be like interrupting a royal speech, thought Paula; Mavis was at her most formidable, and was obviously enjoying having an audience.

"Chris Williams has very kindly agreed to come in for the next few nights," she went on. "He was a hospital nurse before he moved in with Bertie Revelson. He can have Rupert's room."

"Chris Williams," said Paula, glancing across at James, who raised one eyebrow slightly but otherwise did not react. "I didn't know he took on nursing jobs."

"Well, he doesn't really, but he used to work in a mental hospital. Bertie had a bit of a nervous breakdown, you know. His daughter came to stay for a while but found she couldn't cope. After a series of unsatisfactory attendants they found Chris, and after that, Bertie never looked back. It was the end of his painting, though," added Mavis thoughtfully. "He recovered from the breakdown, but he never produced another picture. Rather a pity."

She shifted in her chair as if her back was paining her. Tough she may be, thought Paula, but she really does look very old tonight.

"You think Revelson might have done some more good work?" suggested James.

"Yes, definitely," replied Mavis. "The breakdown was linked up with some new vision in him, probably a change in his style. He was no Picasso, but he was a great enough artist to branch out into something different quite late in life. Chris's coming stopped all that."

"How can you know that?" asked James. "Did you know Revelson very well?"

"Well enough. There was a big streak of laziness in him. I don't mean laziness in producing works of art. I meant a sort of laziness of spirit. Creative laziness."

Mavis paused to glance round at the three people listening to her.

"You're all looking rather puzzled," she went on. "It does sound rather daft, when you think of the number of pictures he painted. How can I explain what I mean by creative laziness? I've got it myself, you know. I've written nearly one hundred books and shall probably write several more, but they'll all be the same. There was a time when I had the chance of writing something new, something original, but I didn't follow it up."

She paused to sip at the glass of sherry that stood on a table beside her chair.

"It wasn't that I needed to stick to the regular money-earners. I was earning plenty at the time and could easily have afforded to experiment. I had ideas in my head. It was a crisis in my own life that set the ideas simmering, but I let them waste away. I didn't want to be bothered. I preferred to keep to the clear and comfortable roadway rather than blaze a new trail. That's what I call creative laziness."

"Very interesting," said Paula with great sincerity. "You know that James and I are both teachers of English literature, don't you?"

"I'm trying to think of literary examples," said James. "Wordsworth? All his good poetry was written when he was young, then came many years of very indifferent stuff, to put it mildly. I'd always assumed that the writer—or artist—had no choice in the matter, that inspiration just failed. But you are saying that the artist does have a choice."

The discussion continued for some time, and then, in a brief pause, Rupert said rather plaintively, "All you frightfully literary people—I'm getting an outsize inferiority complex, listening to you. Does anybody want any more sherry?"

"No thanks," said Mavis, struggling up out of her chair. "I think I'll be getting home. Give me an arm, Rupert. My arthritis is killing me today."

James and Paula averted their eyes. It was painful to witness the contrast between the frailty of the body and the fierce liveliness of the spirit.

"Don't go away," Rupert called out as he opened the door. "I do want to talk to you. I won't be long."

Paula and James were silent for a moment or two after they had gone. Then James said: "What is her real reason for having Chris in to guard her tonight? Is she scared of Rupert and thinks that Chris will be a protection? Or is she planning to do some detective work of her own?"

"I wondered that myself," said Paula. "The obvious thing is to get an agency nurse. I hate to think of Mavis at the mercy of those two."

Hastily she told James about Melissa leaving the threatening note on the old lawn mower, and seeing Chris and Rupert meet in the early hours of the morning.

"It doesn't make sense," James muttered. "If they wanted to hatch a plot against the old woman they could have done it at any time."

"Unless it was something to do with Bertie Revelson—something that needed two pairs of hands. Shifting heavy objects, for example."

"Pictures? But this nighttime meeting was after Bertie was found dead."

"Oh, I don't know." Paula was feeling frustrated, groping after ideas beyond her reach. "What did you think of Mavis's talk of creative laziness?"

"It wasn't casual chat. She was trying to tell us something."

"I thought so to. But what? About Chris's evil influence on Bertie? Or about the artist himself? He killed himself because he knew he'd never paint again? How could he arrange for a picture to fall on his head?"

"He couldn't. It was an accident."

"Unless somebody deliberately weakened the cords. Anyway, the inquest is next week," added Paula impatiently. "We ought to know then."

"Official verdicts don't necessarily tell the truth," said James gloomily. "Careful—Rupert's coming back."

12

Rupert came into the room, poured out whisky, drank it, poured some more, and sat down heavily.

"How do I get out of this?" he asked, looking appealingly at James. "She's determined to make everybody believe that I fed Mrs. P. an overdose, but she knows I didn't."

"You mean Mavis? Why should she accuse you, and what evidence has she got, one way or the other?" asked James in a very matter-of-fact way.

"I'll tell you," said Rupert in a similar manner. "If I got the old girl to take the wrong pills, then it would have to be at her bedtime. Right?"

"If you say so," said James.

"She always took them with her goodnight milk drink that I brought her. Two. One extra put out for later in the night if needed."

"What are they like?" James sounded very casual. "Tablets or capsules?"

"Tablets. Little pink 'uns. Pink 'uns," repeated Rupert.

His speech sounded slightly slurred now. But that too could be an act, thought Paula, since he's making a great play for James's sympathy.

"Can't show you the bottle," went on Rupert. "They took it away. That little Scottie doctor and the sergeant. Evidence, y'know. Fingerprints. Oh sure! The bottle had my fingerprints. And so did the big bottle." He stretched out a hand for the whisky. "All over it."

Very carefully he refilled his glass. James and Paula glanced at each other. Just let him talk, and James's glance; all right, I leave it to you, said Paula's.

"Great stuff," said Rupert after he had taken another drink. "The old girl liked it too. Just a little tot—last thing at night. Helped the old pills to work—the little pink 'uns. Couldn't sleep, y'see. Poor old dame couldn't sleep. Something on her conscience, eh? Like Lady Macbeth. So I left her some whisky by the bed. Did I? That's what they say. Took the glass away, of course. Put a whole lot of the little pink 'uns in the glass. Let 'em dissolve. Taste 'em? No way. She wouldn't taste 'em."

Rupert slammed his tumbler down on the coffee table, suddenly sat up very straight, and said in a voice that didn't sound the least bit drunk: "Drugs and strong drink. There you have it. A fatal cocktail. That's what they think. That I didn't want to wait any longer for her money. And what do you think, old boy?" He turned to James. "Do you think I did it?"

"I haven't the slightest idea," said James. "I thought you were going to tell us why Mavis knows that you didn't."

"Ah, Mavis the Menace. She's a devil, that old hen. Don't you be sorry for her. She don't need no pity. Mrs. P. now—she was a poor old sod. Very lonely. Very depressed. Nothing in her life but memories of the lovely mansion she shared with the late lamented Mr. P. I told 'em how depressed she was but Mavis told 'em she wasn't. Bugger Mavis. Yes, I must tell you. Think, Rupert, my lad. Get it straight now."

He leaned back and shut his eyes. "Christ! My head's splitting."

James and Paula exchanged a glance that said, "That's not surprising. Let's wait for it."

Rupert opened his eyes and struggled to his feet. "Come and see."

They followed him out of the room and across the landing.

"Exhibit one," he said, pushing open the door opposite. "It's a wonder they didn't lock the room and forbid me to enter it."

As they walked into the bedroom Paula found that she had been subconsciously expecting something dark and cluttered and gloomy. But it was quite different. Bright and spacious, with light floral-patterned curtains and a plain pale green carpet, it looked more like a showroom from a high-class furniture store than a room full of an old lady's memories. One wall was taken up with mirrors and white closet fittings, and the bed opposite was a large low divan.

Rupert walked across to it. "Table here," he said, "with water jug. Clock-radio. Alarm bell to summon me in emergency. In this drawer—" and he pulled it open—"were the tablets. Whisky over there." He indicated a cupboard near the window. "Plus gin, mineral water, fruit juice, glasses, tin of biscuits. Every home comfort, as they say. She could get anything she wanted at any time. Teasmade too, though she never used it. I was the tea-maker."

He was talking quickly and clearly now, Paula noticed. There was no sign of slurred speech, of uncertainty. Had that been an act, then? Or was he perhaps subject to violent changes of mood?

"Yesterday evening," continued Rupert, "at about ten o'clock, Mrs. P. called me in my room in the other house to come and bring her evening drink. This was earlier than usual. If there was no call, I'd bring it at half past ten. When I came, I found her sitting on her bed in her dressing-gown, counting out her tablets. Usually I did this for her. She handed me the bottle to put away, and thanked me as usual, saying she wouldn't be needing anything else. Then she asked me if I slept well at nights. I said I did, normally, and she said, 'You are lucky. Thank you for all you have done for me. You've been a great help.'"

"Was that unusual?" asked Paula, as Rupert seemed to be hesitating about what to say next.

"Very unusual," he said at last. "She hardly ever talked about herself, never about me and my affairs. The lawyers interviewed me for the job. She was the boss, and I carried out instructions."

"So how did you know she was so depressed?"

"I overheard her talking to Mavis sometimes. Mostly about her husband and their beautiful house. Actually she talked to Mavis quite a lot. But not to me. So I was quite surprised when she started asking personal questions—had I got a steady girl friend, what was my ambition in life—that sort of thing. Can't remember what I said. Something noncommittal, I guess. And she said, 'Anyway, you'll have no need to worry about money. Goodnight, Mr. Barstow.'"

"She never called you Rupert?"

"Never. It was quite restful really, this formality. Made no personal demands on you."

"I know what you mean," said James. "So this conversation was so unusual that you are thinking now that she intended to take her own life?"

"That's right. At the time I didn't know what it meant, but now—"

Rupert paused a moment before adding, "Let's get out of this room. I've had enough."

When they were back in Rupert's room, James asked, after a nudge from Paula, "What made you say that Mavis knows you didn't give Mrs. Potts an overdose?"

"Because she called Mrs. P. on the internal phone, just as I was about to leave the room. She must have asked Mrs. P. if I was there, because I heard the reply. 'Yes, he's here, do you want him?' I was at the door, and Mrs. P. looked at me and nodded, and I took this to mean I should go, and as I was leaving I heard her telling Mavis that she was determined to get a good sleep tonight."

Rupert stopped talking suddenly, gave a great yawn, and

said: "Do you mind seeing yourselves out? I'm finished. Too much talk. Thanks and all that. 'Bye."

Feeling more and more puzzled, but glad to go, Paula followed James down the stairs and they paused at the front door.

"We'd better go back through Mavis's house," she said. "Rupert says they hardly ever use this entrance."

James was examining the door. "Two bolts and a chain," he said. "Seems odd to be so security conscious when one can easily get through from the other house."

"The whole place is odd," said Paula, "and Rupert is the oddest of the lot. Did you notice he said that Mrs. Potts always addressed him very formally. But according to Carol she was in the habit of greeting him every morning with 'Thank you, dear boy, how is the weather?'"

"Sounds much more like Mavis."

"That's what I thought. And Carol got it from Chris. Third-hand evidence."

"Come on," said James. "Let's get out of here. I can't stand this place another moment. This is the drawing-room door, isn't it?"

Paula rather wanted to explore the other connecting link, through the kitchen, but James would not wait. They made their way carefully back among the antiques and emerged into the hall of Mavis's house. The front door bell rang as they came through.

"That'll be Chris," said James, pulling a face.

"We'll have to let him in. Mavis is exhausted and Rupert is dead to the world."

"I don't like it."

"Neither do I, but it's not our responsibility."

James pulled open the door.

Chris Williams stood on the step, carrying a small brown leather case, and looking very neat and purposeful in his pale blue sweater and light jacket.

"Well, well," he said, "look who's here."

"We're just leaving," said James irritably.

"So I see." Pale blue eyes surveyed them both with cold enquiry. "Did you receive a royal summons too?"

James pushed past him without speaking, but Paula stopped to say, "Rupert's been showing us round. He seems to be very upset about Mrs. Potts's death."

If she had hoped for some reaction she was to be disappointed.

"Is he?" said Chris with a complete lack of expression.

"Goodnight," said Paula hastily and followed James out into the street.

"Do you want to walk a bit?" she asked when she caught up with him.

"No. Let's go home."

"All right."

Paula said no more. James had sunk into one of his rare sulky fits, and was almost certainly asking himself why they had ever bought the house, and silently cursing her for getting so deeply involved with the neighbours' business. There was nothing to be done but keep quiet until he came out of it. Thank goodness we've got Sally and Sam, she thought as they came into the front hall. She ran to open the kitchen door and they shot out, tumbling over each other, making little welcoming sounds and trying to climb up her legs.

"I'm going to hate having to leave them," said Paula, picking up Sally, "but I've got to lecture at ten tomorrow morning. What's your programme?"

"Seminar at two. I don't need to be in college till then."

"Aren't you the lucky one? D'you want anything to eat now? I don't feel frightfully hungry."

"Neither do I. Cheese sandwich will do. I'll get it."

"Thanks, darling. Same for me."

Paula went into the living-room and examined the remains of the log fire. The ashes were still warm; it could be rekindled. She rather prided herself on her fire-lighting skills, and by the time James came in with the supper tray, the wood was glowing brightly. It was discovered that Sally ate cheddar cheese, but that Sam preferred the Dutch. Not a word was said about recent events in Heathview Villas until two hours later, when James announced that there was a letter he must write before tomorrow.

"I'm sure Rupert is telling the truth," he added as he got up from his armchair. "I'm sorry for that guy. He's not very bright. Somebody with a much better brain than his is making use of him. That's my opinion, love, if you're determined to go on with your detective work. But of course I could be wrong."

After James had left the room Paula sat staring into the dying embers of the fire. Both kittens were now contentedly curled up by her feet. So that was James's opinion. It could be that he was speaking out of a fellow-feeling for Rupert—a man of his own type, the same class as himself—but Paula felt sure there was more to it than that. James did not have her own almost obsessional curiosity about other people's motives and actions, but he was very shrewd. He was not often wrong in his assessment of character.

Rupert as the fall guy. It certainly gave her plenty of food for thought.

13

James soon recovered his equanimity, and even regained some interest in the activity of their neighbours, but Paula was careful never to push the discussions too far. *Your* detective work, he had said, and he meant it. He was not going to go out of his way again to search for the author of the poison-pen letters, but Paula could do as she liked and good luck to her.

So they knew where they stood, and if they were careful there was no reason why this difference of intention should cause any dissension between them.

The house began to feel more and more like home, began to feel lived in, even began to feel loved. Sally and Sam helped a lot. They seemed to be growing bigger every day and they certainly grew more adventurous. The garden was explored, a dead field mouse was produced, and Sam's ear had to be tended after an encounter with a fierce neighbouring tomcat.

James's former cleaning lady, Mrs. Fenwick, agreed to come several mornings a week to keep the place in order, and this helped to establish a routine and create a sense of permanence.

The day of the inquest on Bertram Revelson arrived, and Paula agreed to Jill Race's suggestion that the three of them, Jill, Paula and Chris, should go to the courtroom together. It was a sensible arrangement, since they were all to be called to give evidence, but Paula would have preferred to be alone. Chris positively disliked her, she knew, and any genuine feelings of goodwill that Jill might have felt when Paula and James moved into Heathview Villas had been dispelled by the recent happenings there.

That is so often the case, thought Paula as they sat waiting for the proceedings to begin. You move to a new place where you have a slight acquaintance with somebody and expect to become closer friends with them. But you end up by meeting other people you like better, and that earlier contact fades away.

Jill gave her a nudge. "It's our turn next."

"Yes, I know," said Paula.

"Oh. I thought you'd gone to sleep. You looked very distrait."

Paula forbore to remark that Jill had been so deep in conversation with Chris that it was surprising she should notice how anybody else looked.

"I wonder if we shall hear anything new," she said.

"Chris doesn't think so. It's very straightforward."

This proved to be the case.

The police sergeant described his summons to the house and his findings there. Dr. Montague explained the cause of death and the victim's medical condition. Jill's part was very brief, Paula's even briefer. Even Chris had very little opportunity to indulge his histrionic instincts, although he managed to get in some resentful comments about the expert witness who said that the picture-hanging in the Revelson house was very amateurish and unsatisfactory.

"He wouldn't have that self-portrait touched," protested Chris. "He wanted it as it had always been."

The coroner had to call them to order. The inevitable verdict of accidental death was pronounced, followed by a statement of sympathy with the one surviving relative, the daughter whose interest in the event had not extended to flying over from New Zealand to attend the proceedings, and the next case was called.

It will only warrant a short paragraph in the evening paper, thought Paula as they came away. The obituary notices had appeared just after the death. There might be a few more, and then Bertram Revelson would recede into the realms of art history.

Except for the dealers.

"What's going to happen to all those pictures?" Paula asked as the three of them walked the short distance to where Jill had parked her car.

"That's all been attended to. They'll be sold," said Chris loftily. "Except for the self-portrait. I'm having that. He left it to me as a souvenir."

"And the house?"

"That will be sold too eventually. I've agreed to stay on for the time being and keep it in order for Mrs. Dawkins—that's his daughter. She couldn't be here today but she's coming the week after next. I've never met her. I hope she likes me. Won't it be dreadful if we don't get on well together?"

"You'll get on together," said Jill, to whom this last remark had been addressed. "You'll make sure of that, Chris."

Her tone was quite sharp. This odd intimacy between them, thought Paula, is not entirely to Jill's liking. As they approached the car park, she was wondering what excuse she could make to leave them and make her own way home, when she noticed a black Rover draw out from beside Jill's car and turn towards them. The driver pulled round to get out of their way and then stopped and put his head out of the window.

"Hullo, Paula. I'm going into town. Want a lift?"

It was Gordon Vincent. Paula hesitated only a moment before accepting. "I wanted to go into college later," she said, turning to Jill. "I might as well go now, and I can come back on the underground."

"It's a long walk from Hampstead tube station," said Jill, looking at Gordon without much goodwill.

"I don't mind. It's a nice day," said Paula. "Many thanks for bringing me. See you, Jill. And Chris," she added belatedly.

While they were driving away from the parking lot she said, "Thanks for rescuing me, Gordon. I wasn't enjoying the company. I don't know what I've done to give so much offence, but they certainly don't like me."

"Envy, probably."

"Envy? Of me?"

Gordon laughed. "You're too modest. I'd think it was assumed, except that I have the impression that you are very honest too, so it must be genuine. I can't speak for Chris, although I do believe that he has got a very envious nature, but as for Jill Race—well, of course she envies you. The success of your books, your reputation as a scholar, your handsome and high-class partner, not to mention an attractive personality and outward appearance. Of course she envies you. Poor Jill."

Paula, having acted on impulse to get out of a disagreeable situation, now found herself in one even more disturbing. She muttered something about not knowing Jill very well, and then asked where Gordon was going, and suggested a place where it might be convenient for him to leave her.

This having been settled, and before Paula could decide on a safe topic of conversation, he said, "You've been avoiding me lately."

"Have I?" said Paula. "Purely unintentional, I assure you."

This was clearly not the expected response, and she hastily followed up the very slight advantage gained by asking him if he had been to the inquest.

"I came in late and left early," he replied. "Bertie was a client of ours, but I came largely out of curiosity. It went very much as I had expected."

"You think the verdict was correct?"

"I don't see how they could have brought in any other."

"But verdicts can be wrong," persisted Paula. Now that she was fated to be with Gordon for another twenty minutes or more she might as well make use of the opportunity to continue her own research. "Do you think it really was an accident? Or did somebody deliberately weaken that picture cord?"

"By 'somebody' you no doubt mean Chris Williams. Who else would have had the opportunity? According to the police and the expert witness there was no evidence whatever that anybody had tampered with the hanging of the picture. Nor have we any means of proving that somebody deliberately left it crooked, knowing that Bertie would most certainly go and try to straighten it when he next came into the room. Even if somebody did do that, there was no guarantee that it would deal him a fatal blow, as they say."

"But he was very old and frail. It was bound to hit him and knock him over, and the shock alone—"

"I agree. The odds would be heavily in favour of his dying. One way or another. And if by a miracle he survived, there was no evidence that anybody had intended otherwise. Uncertainties in such cases are always unacceptable to all concerned. The law has decided that it was an accident and I think we would do well to believe in the law in this instance."

Paula was irritated by his condescending manner, but could not deny that he was talking a lot of sense. If Chris Williams really had hastened the end of Bertie Revelson, nobody would ever know unless Chris chose to confess. In other words, it had been the perfect murder.

"These things do happen," said Gordon, reading her thoughts. "Every coroner knows about such cases, but if there's no proof—"

He broke off to brake sharply as a man ran off the kerb and across the road at great risk to himself.

Paula, who had shut her eyes, opened them again and said, "It's a wonder so many of us do still have respect for life and truth nowadays. I'm sure you are right, Gordon. I must stop thinking about it. Does Chris inherit anything? Or should I not ask?"

"Ask me anything you like, dear Paula, and I'll answer if I can. Yes, Chris has a substantial legacy, I believe. I don't actually handle the estate—one of my partners does. The house goes to Bertie's daughter, together with the contents."

"Jill said it was to be sold. That means we shall have new neighbours, James and I."

"New neighbours. Ah yes, the great unknown. The momentous question in Heathview Villas—who are to be our new neighbours? Empires may rise and fall, humankind may conquer the universe, but in comparison with the question of who is going to live next door, that's nothing, absolutely nothing."

They were now stationary at traffic lights: there were at least ten minutes to go before Paula would be getting out.

"I've noticed," she said thoughtfully, "since coming to live in Heathview Villas, that residents complain about the claustrophobic and gossipy atmosphere, but all the same they contribute to it themselves."

"How can they avoid it?" asked Gordon as they moved on.

"By never going out at all, I suppose," said Paula. "Like poor old Mrs. Potts."

"Hardly a practical suggestion for those of us earning our livings. Nor a recipe for a full and interesting life. And it didn't stop her being talked about, did it."

"And creating a rich source of gossip by the manner of her death. I wonder what is going to happen at *that* inquest," said Paula.

Gordon laughed. "You see, you're as bad as the rest of us."

"I'm concerned about Rupert," said Paula defensively.

"Aren't we all. We don't want a murderer in our midst. As

far as I know, there's not been one in Heathview Villas in recent years."

"I wish you wouldn't talk like that, Gordon," cried Paula. "I wouldn't have expected you to join in with the rest of the mob, baying for blood."

"I'm sorry. Very sorry." He took one hand off the steering wheel and held her hand for a moment. "Please believe me when I say I didn't mean to imply that I thought Rupert guilty because I don't."

"I'm relieved to hear it." Paula could still not quite keep the reproach out of her voice. "If Rupert's own lawyers don't believe in him—"

"Please, please," he interrupted. "You know as well as I do that it has nothing to do with it. The job of a defence is to make the evidence of innocence stick, regardless of any personal opinion."

"Of course," agreed Paula, wishing she had not given way to her feelings.

"Anyway, he's not been accused yet and probably never will be," said Gordon. "There just isn't any evidence."

"Unless someone deliberately fabricates some."

"Be careful, Paula, you are coming dangerously near slander."

"Good God!" cried Paula. "If that's being slanderous, what is the position of most of the residents of Heathview Villas? You know as well as I do the stories that are going about. And the person who is chiefly responsible for spreading them. Do you want me to get out here? I thought we said the other side of Baker Street."

Gordon had turned into a quiet cul-de-sac and stopped.

"We'll go on in a moment," he said. "I didn't want to say this while driving. Please, Paula, I do beg you to be careful. Bertie's accident was acceptable, but Mrs. Potts's overdose is another matter. Dr. Montague isn't happy about it, and we all—you and James and I—have a lot of respect for his opinion. And as for Mavis—"

He broke off.

"Yes, Mavis," said Paula. "Why is she making things so difficult for Rupert? I can't believe that she really thinks he gave Mrs. Potts an overdose."

"Neither can I," said Gordon. "I've known Mavis for many years. I think she must be afraid."

"You mean afraid to be in the house with Rupert? Why doesn't she sack him, then?"

"He was employed by Mrs. Potts. The arrangement with Mavis was purely informal."

"On, come on, Gordon! She's only got to ask the lawyers—*your* colleagues—to pay Rupert off or find him another job or whatever. Or she could get the connecting doors blocked up if she wanted, and refuse to let Rupert into her house. There's lots of things Mavis could do. But she doesn't. She leaves Rupert with the free run of both houses, but gets Chris Williams to come and guard her at nights and lets everybody in the Villas know she's doing it. But why?"

"I don't know. I only know she's aged a lot since Mrs. Potts died. She really does look ninety now. And acts it too. We'd better get on." Gordon switched on the engine. "I stopped to give you a warning but we seem to have got sidetracked."

"Who are you warning me against?"

"Anybody and everybody to do with Heathview Villas."

"Yourself included?"

"If you like. I'm serious, Paula. And I like you. Very much. Oh yes, I know you're going to remind me about the way I suggested you and I should get together to try to find out who was writing the anonymous letters. It was rather an obvious way of trying to get to know you better, and you dealt with it as I deserved. I don't know if you are still trying to identify the writer, but I must tell you that I think the police ought to be informed now. There've been two deaths in the Villas, admittedly of old people, but—"

"Do you think the deaths and the letters are connected?" interrupted Paula.

"I don't know," he said irritably, switching off the ignition again. "I only know that I have the feeling of an unscrupulous and malicious mind at work somewhere and it makes me very uneasy to think it could turn its attention to you."

"It already has," said Paula. "I had a poison-pen letter myself. Remember?"

"Yes, and so did I. Two weeks ago. What was the postmark on your envelope?"

"Oh—Hampstead area. North-west London."

"Mine too. Time of day?"

"I can't remember. I'll have to check. It had a second-class stamp."

"So did mine. Please, *please* do take yours to the police now. Ask for Sergeant Cox. I'll do the same. I'm quite sure they'll take it seriously, and they have resources that we haven't got. And if you could persuade Jill to take hers, or get hold of her letter somehow, that would help."

"I'll try," said Paula. "What about Bertie's? No way am I going to approach Chris about it."

"I'll ask him myself. I don't suppose I'll have any success, but I can try. Then there's Mavis."

"And Rupert. I'll ask them if they've had letters if you like."

"And I'll do Annie and Derek. And anyone else I think is a possibility. Thanks, Paula. I'm very grateful to you. Did I ever give you my office phone number?" He produced a card. "Call me there if you have anything to report."

Ten minutes later Paula was sitting in her room at college, staring at her morning mail but not taking in a word of any of the letters. All of her thoughts were occupied with the man from whom she had just parted. He was so different from what he had been on their previous meetings. Very little trace of the arrogance remained, of the supercilious manner, but for this very reason she found him more disturbing.

One can fight the attraction if one doesn't like the personality, thought Paula as she forced herself at last to attend to the agenda for a departmental meeting, but the trouble with Gordon is that I'm actually beginning to like him. Very much indeed.

14

A letter had been misdelivered to Paula's room. Feeling very restless, she decided to take it up to the rightful place herself.

As she was walking past one of the classrooms at the far end of the corridor she heard a great shout of laughter coming from behind the closed door. She paused a moment, smiling to herself. This would be the group of first-year students who James was taking for Elizabethan drama. Of course they were laughing, of course they were happy. James was a wonderful teacher, the best in the department, perhaps in the whole college.

He knew he was, but it did not satisfy him. Good teachers were so undervalued in these days when the first question put to any applicant for a job was "What have you published?" And if the applicant knew how to get on in the academic world, she or he would produce a long list of trivial, third-rate articles, with nothing new to say, but quoting all the right authorities. There was no need to show that they had any teaching ability at all.

And yet James envies them, thought Paula angrily as she returned from her errand. And envies me, too, in his heart.

It was an awareness that was always with her, that she was professionally the more successful of the two of them. They never talked about it, and over the years it had come

to matter less and less. James, without making any great
drama of it, had abandoned all hope of shining in the world
of scholarship, and spent more and more of his energies, and
of the considerable fortune that he had inherited, on
charitable works. The education of children who had special
difficulties was his particular interest at the moment, and he
was actively involved in plans to start a school in the
north-west London area.

This much Paula knew, and now, as she returned rather
more slowly to her own office, she began to wonder whether
she had shown enough interest in James's nonuniversity
activities, or whether perhaps he deliberately did not talk to
her much about them.

She tried to shake off these thoughts. Too much analysing
of a relationship was not good. She and James had always
agreed about that, as about so many other things. As she sat
down at her desk again she found herself longing to go and
talk to him at once, this very moment. It was an urgent need
to reassure herself, to make some gesture to confirm their
life together and their future together. But of course she
couldn't interrupt his class, and by the time it was concluded
she herself would be on the way to give a lecture; and James
was going straight on from college to a meeting of the
committee of his favourite charity, so that they would not be
seeing each other until later in the evening, and how many
variations of thought and feeling and action would they both
have experienced by then?

It's Gordon, said Paula to herself as she began to look
through the notes for her lecture; that's what is the matter
with me. I've got to face it and deal with it. It's unthinkable
that James and I should split up now just when we've at last
decided, after so many years, that we can share a home.

She thought of the house, and of Mrs. Fenwick, who was
probably at this moment hoovering the hall and sending the
kittens scuttling for cover, and the thoughts brought much
comfort. But later on, when the day's work was ended, and

she was walking home from the tube station in the dusk of the October evening, the doubts returned.

That wretched anonymous letter. There had been a phrase in it that had particularly upset her on the first reading because it told something of the truth. It was something about career women who were incapable of feeling, who had no capacity for loyalty and devotion.

Was she really like that?

Paula had rather looked forward to the solitary walk after a day spent talking to people, but now that the moment had come, she found herself suddenly overcome by a fit of depression. At one time in her life such attacks had occurred quite frequently, but in recent years they had become more and more rare.

She quickened her step. This stretch of road was poorly lit, and there were no houses, only trees and rough grass, alongside. Perhaps after all it had not been very sensible to walk alone, when darkness fell so quickly. Plenty of cars drove by, but she was the only pedestrian. How different everything felt when you were on foot, worlds away from all those people in their little motorised boxes. And they too, each one of them, cut off from all the others.

Her gloom deepened. Even the prospect of the warm house and the welcoming kittens did not cheer her. When she heard a voice crying faintly, "Help—please help!" she even thought for a moment that it was her own feelings breaking out into speech. Then the rational self took over. She stood still and listened and the voice came again, louder this time.

Paula looked around. It was quite dark now. She was walking along a narrow footpath at the side of the roadway. To her right the headlamps came and went; to her left there was a short steep slope on which grew trees and bushes.

She took a few steps down the slope and called out: "Where are you?"

It had been a woman's voice. Would she have stopped if it had been a man's? The answer came that on this occasion she would. In these moods of hopelessness one simply did not care what happened.

"Down by the blackberry bush." The voice sounded hopeful, and stronger than before. "I've hurt my ankle. I can't stand up."

"I'm coming," shouted Paula. I know that voice, she said to herself as she made her way carefully down the slope; but what on earth is she doing here at this hour?

"Jill!" she cried as she came up to the dark shape huddled on the ground near the brambles. "Whatever are you—"

"Tell you later," said Jill Race, struggling, with Paula's help, to stand on one leg. "Can you help me home?"

"Of course," said Paula with more confidence than she actually felt, for Jill was tall and considerably overweight, while she herself, though tough and in good condition, was shorter and slighter in build.

Their progress was slow, exhausting and, for Jill, very painful.

"Shall I try to stop a car or go and look for help?" asked Paula at one point. "I'm afraid you might be doing further damage to your ankle."

Jill's response was to cling to her even more closely and to beg her not to go away. "I can't cope with anything more," she added in a barely audible murmur.

"It's all right. I won't leave you. It's not much farther."

They struggled on. I would never have got a driver to stop for us, thought Paula, and I don't know who I could go to for help. James isn't there, Gordon's going to be late too—and as for Chris, no, never. Carol? But surely the girls can't be at home either, with their mother wandering about like this. And what am I going to do with her when I do get her home, her thoughts ran on, if Carol and Melissa aren't there? Chris is bound to turn up. He's on the watch for everything.

They came at last within sight of the streetlamp at the end of Heathview Villas.

"You'll be all right here, Jill," said Paula encouragingly. "I really do think it would be best if I ran home to fetch my car. We don't want to go staggering along the road together with everybody staring at us."

"I'm past caring who sees us," replied Jill. "They'll all know about it in any case. You know what it's like here."

"Just let me get my breath then," said Paula.

It was a relief to stand still for a moment or two. The strain of supporting Jill's weight was becoming very arduous. But at least it had cured Paula's depression. All feelings of guilt, self-doubt and apprehension had faded away.

"Why were you there, Jill?" she asked as they moved on again, even more slowly than before. "Whatever is the matter?"

Jill seemed to have gained some strength from the pause and from the prospect of imminent relief. "Melissa's vanished," she muttered. "I was out looking for her."

"Vanished? What do you mean?"

"She went out this afternoon with her friend Roger. That was hours ago. He came back about half-an-hour after they left and said they'd had a violent quarrel and she had gone off in a rage to walk across the Heath by herself."

Jill paused to draw breath and to rest again. There was pain both of mind and body in her voice and in her movements when she went on.

"She hasn't come back. Roger went in one direction to look for her and I went another. We know the paths she was likely to take. But I tripped and fell." Jill gave a little gasp as she leaned too heavily on the injured ankle. "God knows how much longer I'd have been there if you hadn't come along! Nobody ever *walks*—and you try to get a car to stop!"

"I know," said Paula sympathetically. "But Jill, Melissa's old enough to look after herself. She's probably gone to visit friends. Have you tried any of them? Sylvie, for instance?"

"She's not with Sylvie, nor with anybody else I know of. She's never done this before. Paula, I'm worried, I—I—"

Again Jill made a rash movement and became temporarily speechless.

"Don't try to talk now," said Paula. "We'll soon be home and can discuss what to do then."

In silence they made their slow and awkward way past the houses on Paula's side of Heathview Villas. Nobody was about. It was past the usual hour for homecomers from work, but evening visiting had not yet begun. Carol came running down the steps of Number 10 as Jill and Paula came through the garden gate. She was agitated, almost tearful, not at all her usual brusque and confident self.

"Mother!" She put her arms round Jill and clung to her. "What's happened? Chris is here, telling me all sorts of horror stories and I can't get rid of him, and I've had the weirdest phone call from Melissa."

"Melissa!" Jill let go of Paula and held on to Carol instead. "You've spoken to her?"

"Yes. Just now. She sounded—she sounded—I don't know if she was giggling or crying. She only said she was with friends and wouldn't be back tonight and not to worry. And to tell *you* not to worry."

"You're quite sure it really was Melissa?"

"Oh Mum!" Carol sounded reproachful; she was obviously beginning to recover. "What's the matter with you?" she went on as Jill tried to take a step forward and nearly fell.

"She's hurt her ankle. Quite badly, I'm afraid," said Paula. "I think you'd better phone your doctor right away. We'll probably have to get her to hospital for an X-ray."

This news completed Carol's recovery. Give her a practical job to do and she's fine, thought Paula. Aloud she said, "Can you manage now, Carol? I'd like to go home, but I'm not going out again, and I'll be there if you need me."

Paula was feeling very tired indeed. The day seemed to have been going on for a very long time, and she was longing to be in her warm and peaceful home with only the kittens for company. But mother and daughter both begged her to stay.

"If you don't mind," added Carol.

They went into the untidy living-room. Carol cleared a chair and helped her mother to sit as comfortably as she could. Jill leaned back and closed her eyes.

"I'll call the doctor now," said Carol, crouching down by Jill's chair and picking up the telephone extension.

Paula, very glad to rest, took a seat near to them.

Carol was still waiting for a reply when Chris came hurrying into the room.

"What's happening? Why didn't you call me? I only went to the bathroom. Jill! What's the matter—are you ill?"

He was at his most histrionic. Carol waved an arm at him as if trying to drive him away. She had got through to the doctor now and was explaining what had happened. Paula got reluctantly to her feet. She would have to do something about this, get rid of him somehow.

But Jill forestalled her. She opened her eyes, pulled herself upright in her chair, held onto the arms and shouted at Chris.

"Go away! Get out of my house and stay out, you mean sneaky little bastard! Get out and never come back. And do what you bloody well like with that letter. I don't care. I don't *care*!"

She stared at him for a moment, then fell back exhausted and burst into tears. Carol put down the phone and turned to Chris. Her voice was icy when she spoke: "You heard what my mother said."

There was a moment of total silence, and then Chris said very quietly: "She's going to regret this. You are all going to regret this."

He turned and left the room. A moment later they heard the front door slam.

15

There was silence for a moment or two after Chris had gone. Then Paula spoke: "What did the doctor say, Carol?"

"Take Mum to hospital straight away and then call her again."

Jill began to protest. "I don't want to go to hospital if they're going to keep me in."

"They won't keep you in," said her daughter sharply. "They don't keep anybody in unless they're dying, and sometimes not even then."

"Do you want me to drive you?" asked Paula.

"Thanks, I can manage. I've got my licence. We'll be all right now. Thanks again for rescuing my erring parent."

Paula stood up. A few minutes ago she had been longing to escape, but the dramatic departure of Chris had produced a change of feeling in her. "Do what you like with that letter," Jill had said. What letter? It couldn't be the poison-pen one. Surely this must be something different.

Paula's curiosity was aroused. She almost wished that Carol was not there. Jill in her defiant desperation was in the mood to talk, and a tedious wait in a hospital casualty department was conducive to confidences. However, there was nothing to be done about it now, and after assuring Carol that she would be available all evening if needed, and that in any case she would want to know how Jill was, Paula

121

returned home to be welcomed by Sally and Sam and to sit down to a solitary meal.

It's strange, she thought as she turned the omelette out onto a plate, I used to like eating by myself and reading or listening to the radio, but now I'm really missing James badly. Strange but at the same time reassuring. Of course she wasn't going to start up anything with Gordon. It was just one of those things that happened from time to time.

When the phone rang she hurried to answer it, grateful for the interruption. A voice said, "Is that Professor Paula Glenning?"

It was a high, unnatural-sounding voice that could have been male or female.

"Who is that?" asked Paula sharply.

"Have you forgotten what you read in your letter?" asked the voice.

"Who is that? Who are you?"

Paula knew that it was pointless to ask, but could not stop herself.

A high laugh came over the line.

"It's an offence to make anonymous phone calls," snapped Paula.

The laugh came again and then the line went dead.

Without any hesitation Paula called the number of the local police station and asked for Sergeant Cox. Her luck was in. He was available and willing to listen. Paula, summoning up all her powers of concise and clear exposition, told him about her own poison-pen letter and the others that she knew of for sure, apologised for not having informed the police earlier, and went on to describe the phone call.

"Can you trace it?" she concluded.

"It depends. We'll do what we can. And I'd like that letter, please, Professor, as soon as possible."

"Tonight?"

"Tomorrow morning will do." There was a pause. Paula half expected a reproach for not having reported it before, but none came. "Would it be convenient if I called on you about half past nine?"

"That'll be fine," said Paula. "I don't have to go out till later. Thank you very much."

She put down the phone with a feeling of relief, but almost immediately she picked up the phone again as a sudden thought struck her.

Could it have been Chris, doing one of his melodramatic acts? Jill's defiance must have infuriated him; he would want to hit back somehow. Should she tell the sergeant of her suspicion?

An urgent desire to talk to James about it came over her. If he had answered the call he would have been forced to slacken his determination to remain detached from the whole business.

For about half a minute she stood with the telephone in her hand, restless, uncertain, wondering what was the matter with her. Finally she replaced the receiver and made herself sit down on the sofa to watch the television news. Sam and Sally, blissfully and deeply asleep after much activity, lay curled up together at the other end of the sofa.

Paula regarded them with envy.

When the telephone rang again she reached for it at once. In her present mood even mysterious calls were better than nothing.

It was Gordon, asking if she had anything new to report. She told him briefly about Jill's accident and the phone call and her talk with the police sergeant.

"I've learned something too," he said, "but I'd rather not tell you over the phone. May I come round for half an hour?"

Paula hesitated. James would not be home for at least another hour, but on the other hand it was better not to take the slightest risk that he might find Gordon there.

"I'd rather come round to your place," she said. "I need a change of scene."

How idiotic that sounded! She had been out most of the

day, as he must well know. Any friendship that might
develop with Gordon beyond the social round of the Villas
must be founded on truth, not on this sort of pretense. She
shut the front door behind her and stood just outside it on
the step, heartily wishing she had not said she would go.

Perhaps she had better call him back and say she had to
stay at home. After all, she had promised Carol that she
would be in all evening. A promise was sacred to Paula.
How could she have forgotten it, even momentarily?

Perhaps she had better leave a note in Jill's letterbox to
say where she was. But she wouldn't be gone for long, and
they would have to wait ages at the hospital. One always did
have to.

Slowly she came down the steps and walked towards the
front gate, very annoyed with herself for her indecision, but
at the gate she paused again and stood there holding it open
and thinking how much she liked its Victorian wrought-iron
work, one of the many attractive features of the house,
indeed of the whole street. But if she and James had known
just how deeply they would have become involved in their
neighbours' affairs, then maybe . . .

Maybe they ought to have bought one of those "elegant
new town houses" nearer in to the West End. Much smaller
rooms, of course, and low-ceilinged, but well-designed and
quite attractive. On the other hand, the gardens had been
very small, and the battery of security devices on the gates
and walls had aroused all Paula's claustrophobic tendencies,
and she knew how much James loved the old and spacious
and genuine, as indeed she did herself, and so when the
opportunity arose . . .

With her thoughts roaming happily over their first view-
ing of Number 12 Heathview Villas, Paula had momentarily
forgotten her own errand and was startled to hear a man's
voice nearby.

"Waiting for somebody?"

It was Rupert Barstow. He must have approached very

speedily and silently. But from which direction had he come?

"No," she replied, very grateful to have her paralysis of indecision brought to an end. "I'm just dithering because I'd promised to be at home in case Carol Race needed me but I've also said I'll go and collect some information that Gordon Vincent has got for me."

"Is it very urgent information?"

"It can wait."

"Then may I suggest a solution? Why don't you phone him to say you'll collect it tomorrow?"

Paula laughed. "That's what I'd just decided. Are you in a hurry, Rupert? Would you like to come and join me for a cup of coffee? James is at a committee meeting but he won't be very much longer."

The invitation clearly brought as much relief to him as his arrival had brought to her. Paula left him tentatively making friends with the kittens and used the extension in the kitchen to call Gordon.

She was very brief. "I'm sorry, but something's cropped up. I'll have to make it tomorrow evening. What time do you get home?"

Gordon obviously thought, as she had intended he should, that James had returned earlier than expected. They arranged for her to call in the following evening soon after six, and then he added, speaking very urgently, "Do take care. You remember our conversation this morning."

"Of course."

"And the person we were talking about?"

Paula hastily cast her mind back. "The caretaker-housekeeper?" she said.

"That's the one. Please be very cautious."

"Thanks, I will," she said. "See you."

He means Rupert, she said to herself as she put down the phone; we were talking mainly about Mavis and Rupert. What has Gordon discovered? Has Rupert just been to see him?

Oh, this is intolerable, she thought as she tipped an assortment of biscuits out onto a plate, this having to suspect everybody all the time! Gordon is warning me against Rupert, and I suppose I'm now going to have Rupert warning me against Gordon, or against Mavis or Chris or somebody else. We just can't live here in this atmosphere any longer. If it doesn't get sorted out soon James and I will have to move. Whatever the cost and inconvenience we'll just have to buy another house somewhere else and sell this one.

And I absolutely refuse to be afraid of Rupert Barstow, she thought defiantly as she carried the tray into the living-room; and anyway, James likes him and won't in the least mind his being here when he comes home.

"What's this about Carol Race needing help," said Rupert as he took his coffee mug off the tray.

Paula explained about Jill's accident.

"It's lucky for her you were walking home," was Rupert's comment.

"I suppose she could have crawled up to the side of the road, and eventually somebody would have stopped to help."

"Maybe. I wouldn't have wanted to count on it. And in any case it's a bit daft to go looking for somebody on Hampstead Heath—needles in haystacks, you know, that sort of thing."

"That was rather my own opinion," agreed Paula, "but Jill did say that Melissa had her favourite places—an oaktree where she'd once carved her initials on the trunk, for instance."

"Oh, well," said Rupert, stroking Sally's ears. After a pause he added, "I hope she's all right. Melissa, I mean. The Heath gets its full quota of murders and rapes nowadays."

"She phoned home," said Paula. "Carol took the call. She said she was staying with friends, but didn't say who they were."

"Perhaps she's been kidnapped," suggested Rupert.

"Do you know, I actually wondered that myself. Quite seriously, I mean."

"Did she say anything about ransom money?" Rupert sounded amused.

"Jill hasn't got any money. I was thinking of—oh, it does sound silly!—I was thinking somebody might want to stop her doing something or saying something." Paula laughed. "It doesn't need James to tell me my imagination runs out of control. I know it does. Would you like some more coffee?"

"Yes please," he said, holding out his mug.

Paula was struck by something young and appealing in the gesture. He's lonely and unhappy, she thought as she got up to go to the kitchen, and I don't believe he's the brash opportunist he seems to be pretending to be.

When she came back she said, "Can't you find another job, Rupert? Something with more independence, and more congenial?"

"It was difficult enough before," he muttered. "It's going to be ten times more difficult now."

"Not necessarily," said Paula, beginning to feel a little irritated by his defeatist attitude. "I know it's miserable for you at the moment, but the gossip will eventually die down and you've got good friends. Surely Mrs. Potts's lawyers will be able to help you. And your referees. Presumably you had to produce some good references to get the job."

"Yes," said Rupert, staring at his coffee mug. "They were quite a work of art. I forged them."

"Why?" demanded Paula, and then, as he did not instantly respond, she added impatiently, "Come on, Rupert. You'll have to tell me all about it now. I shan't tell anybody except James, and you know he's to be trusted. The honour of the old school tie, that sort of thing."

"I like James," said Rupert. He finished his coffee, put the mug down heavily on the table, picked up Sam and stroked his ears in a steady, very controlled movement as he talked.

"I'm an illegitimate son of a peer of the realm—a very old title, not one of your new creations."

He mentioned a name. "Never heard of them," said Paula.

"No, you wouldn't. They don't produce revolutionary politicians or drug-pushers or strings of unsavoury divorces. Very unnewsworthy, my folks are. Very conscientious and traditional. I was brought up by foster parents who were cousins of my natural father."

"Your mother?"

"My mother dumped me at a very tender age on the doorstep of the ancestral home and was never heard of again."

Rupert began to laugh. "If you submitted the story of my life to a publisher of romances, they'd reject it as being exaggerated. I'll tell you sometime if you're interested. The thing I'm trying to tell you now is that I was twice chucked out of a school for being violent and disruptive, and on two other occasions I attacked my foster parents so viciously that I narrowly escaped being sent to an institution for juvenile delinquents, but a kindly psychiatrist stepped in and got me transferred to a special school that he was interested in and that was my salvation. I became their star pupil and was actually quite happy for some years. Am I boring you?"

Paula had lit a cigarette and was staring at him intently. "On the contrary. But I wish James was here. He'd be very interested indeed. In your special school, I mean. It's his main interest outside college nowadays—he's involved in the setting up of one."

"Don't tell him!"

Rupert's whole attitude changed dramatically at Paula's remark. From being relaxed and confiding he became tense, watchful, suspicious. "Can't you understand?" he snapped. "I don't want to be patronised—looked on as a case for special treatment. I've had enough."

"I'm very sorry," said Paula. "Of course I understand. That was thoughtless of me. I promise not to tell him, Rupert, and I do appreciate your confidence. May I ask whether your present employers—Mrs. Potts's lawyers— know anything of your history?"

"Not a thing. The school kept me on as a member of staff when I reached the age to leave, and I stayed there for some years teaching English and producing plays and coaching tennis players and other sports jobs. They'd have kept me on indefinitely, but I felt I ought to try to go it alone."

"You mean break out from the sheltered environment? That was brave of you," commented Paula.

"It wasn't too bad at first. I got a job in a place that was sort of on the fringe of the public school system and did all right there. Then I tried moving up-market, but that was a disaster. Somebody found out my history and I was asked to leave. Very politely. They didn't want a scandal. That's when I started faking a life. It's surprisingly easy. I'd done it twice, for temporary jobs, and did it on a rather more grand scale for the Mrs. Potts job."

"Which brings us up to date," said Paula. "Yes. I see. Very clearly indeed. A rich old woman's doubtful death is the last thing you need. Have the police questioned you, Rupert?"

"Naturally. As far as I can tell, they accept my false position. The lawyers back it up, of course."

"What about the faked references?"

"So far they haven't been questioned. But if the inquest doesn't result in a convincing verdict of accident or suicide, then it's all up with me."

Paula lit another cigarette. "You know what I'm going to advise, don't you?" she said presently.

"Yes. To tell the truth at once."

"Well?"

"I know it. I don't know whether I can do it."

"It couldn't be worse than what might happen if you don't. And the longer you leave it—"

"I know, I know."

"I can't persuade you to let me tell James? He's enormously helpful in emergencies. And he likes you very much."

"Because I like jazz and he thinks I'm a fellow public schoolboy."

"Jazz, yes. I wouldn't say the other mattered so much. There he is."

Paula jumped up and ran out into the hall to greet James with exceptional enthusiasm.

"Why this ardour?" He fended her off in order to take off his raincoat.

"Rupert's here. I'm going to make some more coffee."

"China tea!" he called after her as she ran off to the kitchen.

Through the open doors she could hear Rupert saying that he must go now and leave them in peace.

"Oh don't go," said James warmly. "You're just the man I wanted to see. You know about sports equipment, don't you? What do you think it would cost to—"

Paula listened no longer. She did a little dance of triumph around the kitchen and took as long as she possibly could to prepare the tea tray.

16

"Did he tell you?" Paula asked James an hour later, immediately after they had said goodnight to Rupert.

"He did indeed, in spite of your very clumsy excuse for leaving us alone together."

"It wasn't an excuse and it wasn't clumsy. I really wanted to know if Jill was back from hospital."

"Jill at hospital?" echoed James.

"I'd forgotten you didn't know. Can you bear to hear about it?"

"I can indeed. I'm getting rather tired of being protected from the Heathview Villas gossip as if it were not a fit subject for my tender ears."

"And I'm getting rather tired," Paula snapped back, "of being shut out of what really matters to you and having to hear about it for the first time from a comparative stranger."

"Yes, I see," said James after a moment's pause. They had returned to the living-room and were standing glaring at each other. "Do we have to have a quarrel now," he went on. "It seems such a waste of time."

Paula began to laugh. "You're dead right. It is. I'm sorry."

"And I'm sorry too."

"Okay. You start."

James's response was to hand over the thick wadge of papers that he had brought back from his committee

131

meeting. There was silence in the room while Paula studied the documents with great care.

At last she looked up and said, "James, this looks super. How far have they got?"

"They'll start work on the alterations to the house next month. We hope to be in business by the spring."

"Thanks for showing me." Carefully she tidied up the papers she had been studying and handed them back to him. "I like the sports centre," she said. "I suppose there wouldn't be—"

She broke off. She had been about to say, "A job for Rupert," but was afraid of seeming to interfere.

James finished the sentence for her. "We've been talking about it, Rupert and I," he added. "Of course there can't possibly be any firm promise, but personally I think he'd do very well. They're going to need somebody who has a first-hand experience of the sort of problem the students have had to face."

"If only he could get clear of this present mess. What did you advise him to do?"

"One can't advise, love. It's up to him to decide."

"It's bound to come out," said Paula unhappily. "Past history of violence, faked references. Even if they don't manage to prove that he drugged the old woman, it'll be the finish of any career that he might take up. What *can* he do, James?"

They discussed it for some time but could come to no hopeful conclusion.

"I suppose he'll have to tell Mrs. Potts's lawyers," said Paula doubtfully. "Maybe they can advise him."

"I'd feel happier about that," said James, "if it were any other firm than that of your friend Gordon. I don't trust that guy an inch."

"Oh James darling, neither do I!" burst out Paula. "What am I going to do about him? *Please* help. He's making a pass at me and I'm scared stiff I'm going to do something silly."

She spoke on impulse, without a moment's reflection, but after she had spoken she looked at James very anxiously. How would she react, she found herself wondering, if her partner said he was very attracted to another woman and wanted her help in resisting it? Would she be angry, would she be flattered? What an extraordinary situation to get into! They were talking in a way they had never talked before in all these years together.

Well, there was no going back now.

James was speaking, rather tensely. "Of course if you really like the guy—"

"I don't!" almost shrieked Paula. "I mean I do, of course, in a way. Otherwise it wouldn't arise. But I don't *want* to."

"You'd better go and have an affair with him."

"I don't want to! I'm asking you to help me stop *now*. Before it goes any farther."

"How can I help? You're the one who has to do the stopping."

"Yes, I know, I must be crazy. But you know—"

Paula broke off and actually clamped a hand across her mouth to prevent herself from saying the words that had sprung to her mind. She had been about to remind him of the times when he had been the one to do the straying. That would be fatal. They had always managed to avoid that sort of tit-for-tat recrimination.

What could she say now, how could they get back to that deep community of feeling they had experienced while discussing Rupert's problems? If only she hadn't spoken! But it was James's fault. He had invited it by the tone of voice in which he had said "your friend Gordon."

There was no solution to her present problem, and now was the moment to let it alone. But oh, the difficulty of letting things alone once they had been stirred up. How wise she and James had been over the years never to discuss their relationship and how stupid of her to have broken the rule. But not only stupid of me, she hastily corrected her thoughts; it's his doing as well, he asked for it. "Your friend Gordon." I refuse to take all the blame myself.

The cats, disturbed by the tension in the room, were demanding to be let out, and Paula was grateful for the excuse to get up and open the door. She then fetched a cigarette, lit it, and returned to her chair. "I'd better tell you about Jill's accident," she said, "and bring you up to date with the affairs of Heathview Villas."

"And the inquest on Revelson," James reminded her.

"Good Lord, was that really only this morning!" exclaimed Paula. "It feels like days ago. All right, let's start at the inquest. The verdict was accidental death."

Paula spoke quickly and confidently. This was an easy task, a straightforward account of the day's events. Even the rescue by Gordon from Jill and Chris, and their subsequent conversation in his car, presented no great problem once she was launched on her expository style, omitting all feelings, confining herself purely to the facts.

"That's why," she concluded, "I really did need to leave you and Rupert alone while I went to see if Jill was home."

"And was she?"

"Yes, being put to bed by Carol. She's got a haematoma—a very deep bruise, almost more painful than a break, but it won't take so long to heal."

"And was there any news of the other girl—Melissa?"

"Apparently not. But she had phoned once already, so Carol said."

"You don't think it's possible that Melissa made that phone call to you?"

"No, we're on good terms now. It might just have been Sylvie, but I think the most likely person is Chris."

"At any rate, it drove you into telling the police. And reporting the letters too. I'm relieved to hear that. Will you go round to Gordon's tomorrow evening to hear what his 'new information' is?"

"Yes, I think so. And try to find out what the warning

against Rupert was all about. Naturally I shall keep an open mind."

"Naturally."

"I mean," Paula ploughed on conscientiously, "that I shall try to discover whether Gordon is deliberately casting suspicion on Rupert in order to divert attention from himself. He—or his law firm—might be up to something shady that Rupert knows about. Or they think Rupert knows about."

"I get the point," said James. "That would let you out nicely, wouldn't it, darling, if your boyfriend turned out to be a crook?"

Paula stared at him for a moment and then began to laugh.

"Do you think he's a crook?" she asked.

"I do indeed. I thought so from the first."

"Evidence," she demanded.

"Sheer prejudice," he admitted.

"Now wait a minute," said Paula. "Let's look at this sensibly. Opinion as to his merits as a lawyer seems to be divided in the Villas. Bertie Revelson, Mavis, and Mrs. Potts are—or rather, were—all clients of his, presumably satisfied ones. Jill Race is anti-Gordon, though Carol thinks he might be able to help her mother to maximise her income. Are there some suspect financial dealings? What do you think, James?"

"I'm sure of it. But, as I told you, it's sheer prejudice."

"Do we know about anybody else?"

"The television couple seemed to be friends of his."

"That doesn't mean they'd trust him with their affairs. How about Chris Williams?"

"Presumably he's pro-Gordon, since he was Bertie's lawyer."

"It doesn't follow," said Paula. "I've got a feeling that Chris isn't one of Gordon's fans. Something I've heard, or some impression I gained from somebody. Can't put my finger on it at the moment. What do you think Dr. Montague thinks of Gordon?"

"I haven't the slightest idea," replied James, "but I'd like to see the Montague doctors again. Weren't we going to invite them to dinner?"

"Let's fix it now." Paula got up to let in the kittens, returned from their evening excursion and now very happy to settle down on the appropriate laps. With some difficulty Paula studied her diary.

"We can't phone them at midnight," protested James.

"No, but we can look at dates."

They did this, very contentedly, discovering by the way that there was a concert at the Royal Festival Hall the following Sunday that they had booked for a long time ago and forgotten about. This started up an argument that cropped up from time to time as to the best recording of the Mozart G Minor Symphony, and since neither the composer nor the conductors and orchestras in question were present to plead their cause, and since neither of the disputants would ever admit the validity of the other's opinion, the discussion took its usual inevitable course.

Sam resettled himself and Sally began to wash vigorously. The hands of the wall clock moved on to a quarter to one. A couple of hours ago Paula would never have believed it possible that the evening could end so happily.

17

Paula duly handed over the poison-pen letter to Sergeant Cox the following morning, and then, having a couple of hours to spare before she need set out for central London, decided to call on Jill.

She collected some magazines and a bunch of chrysanthemums and rang the doorbell of Number 10 rather tentatively, hoping that Carol had arranged to stay at home herself or had arranged to have somebody stay with her mother. To her relief the door was opened almost immediately. Melissa stood there, looking very tousled and agitated.

"I was just going to have a bath," she said. "Are these for Mother?"

"May I come in? Or is it inconvenient?"

It was a wet and windy morning, and Paula was not getting much shelter as she stood on the doorstep.

"Oh yes. Sorry." Melissa moved out of the way. "Carol's gone to school," she went on as she shut out the weather. "I said I'd stay at home today. Would you like some coffee?"

"No thanks," replied Paula to this half-hearted offer, "but I'd like to talk to you if I may."

"Oh. Yes. Well, I guess I can have my bath later."

Melissa moved into the living-room. It had been untidy enough the previous time Paula had seen it, but that was nothing to its present condition. Surely only burglars in a very great hurry could produce such extreme chaos.

"Sorry," said Melissa, collapsing onto a heaped-up chair and waving her arm vaguely in the direction of another such. "I can't handle it. I can't handle anything."

"Would *you* like some coffee?" suggested Paula.

"P-please," spluttered Melissa through a succession of sobs. "No, I'd rather have hot chocolate," she said more distinctly. "There's some in the cupboard by the sink. It's—it's very kind of you."

These last words sounded oddly formal, coming from Melissa. Paula, telling herself that the girl was much in need of something sweet and childlike for comfort, made her way to the kitchen, which was fully as disorderly as she had expected.

Melissa had calmed down by the time she returned and seemed anxious to talk.

"It's all my fault," she said. "Mum's accident. If I hadn't gone off like that—"

"Luckily there is no great harm done," said Paula. "Your mother will soon be better. By the way, why did you stay away? Was it something special?"

"Not really. I only went with Sylvie to see Gordon's wife, Sylvia. It's not the first time I've been. Don't tell Mum. Nor Carol. They wouldn't approve, but there's no harm in it. She's very glamorous, Sylvia, I mean. She's got lots of model clothes and sometimes she gives me something."

"I see. Is that where you phoned from when you spoke to Carol?"

"That's right. I didn't dare tell her where I was. Sylvia suggested I should stay the night, and Sylvie too, but she had to go home because Gordon gets angry."

"Hold on a minute," said Paula. "I thought Gordon's wife had dumped Sylvie on him and he was annoyed about it."

"Oh no. It's not like that at all. Sylvie is Mrs. Vincent's stepdaughter and they get on quite well. There's no reason why they shouldn't share the flat, but Gordon wouldn't have it. He said he'd lost one housekeeper when his wife left and he was determined to keep Sylvie to do the shopping and cooking. She's quite good at it, by the way."

"I see," said Paula, mentally comparing the two versions of Gordon's domestic affairs. On the whole she was inclined to believe Melissa's version rather than Gordon's. Spite was indeed present, as he had said, but the malice was on his side, not on his wife's. Here was evidence that one could not trust what he said. Could one ever trust his word at all? Probably not.

Tentatively she questioned Melissa further, but the girl seemed to have lost interest in the subject and was intent only on explaining her own actions.

"I was longing to get away from home for a bit. You know how it is. So I thought I'd stay overnight. But I didn't want Mum and Carol to worry. And when I came back this morning—"

A fresh outburst of tears threatened.

"You can make up for it by helping them now," said Paula briskly. "How about starting by tidying up the place a bit. I'm very untidy myself," she added, "but I know it makes life easier if one doesn't live in quite such a mess."

"I know." Melissa took a grip on herself. "Sylvia Vincent's flat is lovely."

"Shall we start now? I've got some time to spare."

Paula's offer, which was gratefully accepted, was not without ulterior motive. Melissa, in her softened and repentant mood, had already let slip one interesting piece of information, and might well say more. It was natural to chat as they hung up coats and jackets and replaced books on shelves, swept up crumbs, and removed a large amount of dirty crockery to the kitchen.

"Thanks for getting rid of Chris," said Melissa at one point in the operations. "Carol says you chucked him out."

"I don't think I did. It was your mother who told him to go."

"But she'd never have done it if you hadn't been behind her."

Paula had to admit that this might be true, but she was rather disturbed to find herself cast in the role of Jill's champion and support.

"Melissa," she said as they were stacking away the dishes they had washed, "what was that last threat of Chris's? Your mother was quite desperate. She said, 'Do what you like with that letter.' And Chris said very nastily, 'You're going to regret this, all of you.' What letter did he mean?"

"The poison-pen one, I suppose. The one we found. We read it together. Don't you remember? About the tax fiddle."

"Of course I remember. But don't you see, it can't have been that one that Chris was referring to. He'd read it, of course, as we had, and maybe other people have read it, and certainly the person who wrote it. But there wouldn't be any point in threatening to make it public if so many people knew about it already."

"He could tell the Inland Revenue," said Melissa doubtfully.

"I doubt if they'd take much notice of statements made in anonymous letters and repeated by a third party. No, I believe there is another letter somewhere—one written by your mother herself—that Chris has somehow got hold of. Something that matters a lot more to her than a tax fiddle. Something that she so much wants not to be made public that she's allowed Chris to bully her and dominate her life to stop him doing it."

Melissa, wiping round the sink, did not immediately respond. At last she said, "Isn't that just making a guess?"

"Did you discuss this possibility with Carol?" countered Paula.

"We did mention it," admitted the girl, "but we didn't have much time this morning."

"And what did Carol think?"

"What you've just said. She's been trying to get Mother to tell her."

"And—?"

"Mum just said Chris was talking about the anonymous letter."

"I see. Do you think your mother would like to see me?"

The girl was not sure. "She was asleep when I went up just now, but maybe she's woken up with all this noise we've been making."

"Then I'll take these flowers up myself. May I use this vase?"

Jill's bedroom was orderly but characterless. Here was a place to sleep and keep one's clothes; there was no sense of a retreat or of any expression of personal taste. Paula found it sad, but at the same time felt irritated.

Jill, propped up in bed, thanked her effusively for the chrysanthemums. "My ankle's much better," she said in reply to Paula's questions. "I'm getting up soon. I can get about provided I hold on to something. Melissa need not have stayed at home."

"I think she's glad to," said Paula. "She feels very guilty."

"There was no need to. And she needn't have done all that clearing up. I'd have done it as soon as I was mobile again."

Paula made a noncommittal reply. This was typical Jill, incapable of generous gratitude, of any kind of warm spontaneous response.

She would never be any different. A good woman by conventional standards, but an unattractive personality. Unlike the two daughters. Perhaps they were like their father, that drunken journalist who went off to California with a wealthy older woman.

Melissa missed him; Carol pretended she did not. It was all terribly sad.

But what on earth could Jill have written that had put her so much at the mercy of Chris's malicious threats? It was impossible to ask her outright, particularly not at this moment when in spite of her injury she seemed as contented as she was ever likely to be with her life. She was receiving sympathy and attention; both daughters were very concerned, and she was also getting a rest, which she badly needed.

"I'm going to college later this morning," said Paula. "Is there anything you'd like me to take or fetch or do? What about your classes?"

Jill had a little list of instructions that she had prepared for Melissa. She handed it to Paula instead, and this time her gratitude seemed rather less grudging.

"That's a weight off my mind. There is one other thing—but I can't ask you or anybody else to do it for me," she concluded.

"What is it?" asked Paula.

"I want to get the keys of this house back from Chris. I don't at all like the thought that he can come in at any time, particularly when I'm laid up like this."

"I wish I could help," said Paula sympathetically, "but I'm afraid it wouldn't be any good my asking him."

Should she, after all, ask Jill outright what Chris's threat meant? Perhaps it would be best to wait and see what Jill said.

"I don't think it's much good anybody asking him. Carol is going to have a try—he's a little bit afraid of Carol. So am I, to tell the truth. She's got a temper, not a quick flare-up that's soon over, like Melissa, but an explosion of long-suppressed feeling that can be quite alarming."

Paula listened with interest to the girls' mother talking about them in this comparatively relaxed manner.

"Melissa seems to be in a very contrite mood," she said when Jill paused.

"It won't last," said Melissa's mother.

Evidently there were to be no confidences about Chris.

"I'll just have to change the locks," said Jill as Paula got up to go. "It's a nuisance and an expense, but I'll see to it as soon as I'm a little more mobile."

If I were you I would see to it today, thought Paula; I'd phone a locksmith, or get Melissa to do so. Afterwards she was to wish that she had said this aloud, and had pressed the matter, but maybe it would not have made all that much difference.

She said goodbye to Jill and her daughter, who in a fit of enthusiasm was now scrubbing out the bathroom, and left the house with a sense of dissatisfaction, as if she was hovering around the answers to some of her questions but could not quite grasp at them. Feeling the need for a little air and exercise, and still having a little time to spare, she decided to walk through the narrow passage which led out onto the Heath.

The rain had temporarily stopped, and the wind, in Paula's restless mood, was invigorating. Beyond the shelter of the garden walls, however, it became too strong for comfort, and she decided to walk round the boundary fence of Mavis's garden instead of venturing further into the open. The fence was high, but a slight rise in the ground a few feet away enabled her to see over it. She scrambled further up the slope to get a better view of the back of the long white house, and stared across at it.

The house—or rather the two houses—looked much the same from the back as from the front: plain and angular. Paula identified the window of Rupert's room in Mrs. Potts's dwelling, then turned her eyes to Mavis's side.

Which of those windows was that of Rupert's bed-sit? And did Mavis sleep in the large front bedroom, as had her neighbour?

As Paula stood looking, steadying herself by clinging to the trunk of a small silver birch tree, a light came on at one of the windows at the back. The window was uncurtained, the light shone clearly on this dark morning, and Paula had a good view of a considerable section of the room.

She could also probably be seen by anybody who chose to look in her direction. Paula quickly got behind some bushes. She had wandered off the footpath and scrambled up a slope full of prickly undergrowth, and if anybody challenged her it would be difficult to deny that she was spying. Nobody out for a casual stroll would end up in such a position.

The person who had switched on the light came closer to the window and looked out. Paula, crouching low and peering between branches, was sure that she could not now be seen.

It was a woman at the window, tallish, slim, with short, well-cut straight hair. At such a distance it was impossible to guess her age, but Paula was sure that she was not very old.

Who could she be? One of the agency staff, come to clean and cook? Or perhaps Mavis's secretary. Paula decided on the latter. The room looked like an office. The woman had sat down at the desk by the window, and on the desk was a low keyboard and a small screen.

Mavis's secretary was typing her latest novel on a word processor. So what was remarkable in that, Paula asked herself, and the answer soon came: Nothing remarkable, except that Mavis had said that her secretary was old *and* old-fashioned and insisted on using a little old electric typewriter.

So what? Mavis had got another secretary. It was nothing to get excited about, certainly nothing to make it worth while to crouch here in great discomfort among damp and prickly bushes.

And yet it nagged at Paula's mind as she made her way back home.

18

Paula collected her briefcase, which she had left ready on the hall table, and walked across the road to where she had parked her mini. She had opened the door of the passenger seat and was putting the case down when she saw Annie, the former television cook, doing the same thing a few yards farther along the road. She smiled a greeting and Annie came towards her.

"We haven't seen much of you lately," she said. "How are you liking life in Heathview Villas?"

"Fine, on the whole," replied Paula brightly. "Only there does seem to be rather a large number of deaths."

Annie frowned. "Mrs. Potts. And who else? Oh yes. Bertie Revelson, of course. But they were both pretty ancient."

"Yes, I know, but let's hope it doesn't go in threes."

Annie stared at her. "Who are you talking about?"

"Nobody in particular. Sorry. Forget it. By the way, did you and Mavis get together over that book you mentioned at Gordon's party?"

"You mean me illustrating a story of hers? Yes, we're working on it now."

Paula was rather surprised. As far as she could recollect, the project had not sounded as if it had got that far. She made some polite enquiries. It turned out that they really were working closely together, discussing the text and the pictures for each chapter before the work was actually carried out.

"So you are round at Mavis's place quite a lot," Paula said casually. "Or does she come to you?"

"She comes to me. She likes a chance to get out."

"Can she really walk so far?" exclaimed Paula in some surprise.

"She probably could if she had to," was Annie's reply, "but actually Rupert drives her. Or rather, he used to, but this week she's insisted on me going to fetch her, which is a bit of a nuisance."

"She does seem to have taken against Rupert since Mrs. Potts died," said Paula. "James and I have noticed it. You don't think he could possibly have had anything to do with her death, do you, Annie?"

"Of course not," was the brisk reply. "Mavis's imagination is running away with her. If she doesn't want Rupert in the place then she's only got to tell Mrs. P.'s lawyers."

"That's what we thought. Not that it's any of our business," added Paula.

"But it is of mine. This book means a lot to me, and I don't want anything happening to Mavis before it's finished," said Annie.

"And after that she can kill herself or get murdered or whatever she likes," said Paula with a faint smile.

Annie made a grimace. "It does sound selfish. But you know what I mean."

"I do indeed. Good luck to you."

Paula was about to get into her car. She could not think of any way to gain further information from what had to appear to be a casual conversation, but it seemed that Annie had something more to say.

"Paula, you've got me worried. Or rather, I was worried before, but your saying 'it goes in threes' only confirms my worry. There's something very wrong with Mavis. She's not concentrating in the way she's always been able to. She's scared, or she's sick. Or *something*. Can't you find out? She won't talk to me about it and I can't get anything out of Rupert. Neither can Derek. Can't James help? We had the impression that he and Rupert were quite pally."

Paula promised to do her best to find out what was the matter with Mavis. "By the way," she added as if as an afterthought, "has she got a new secretary? I'm sure I remember her saying that her secretary was old and old-fashioned, but I saw quite a youngish woman around her place just now, who didn't look like one of the agency cleaners or cooks, and I wondered—"

"Yes, she has," Annie broke in. "That's another thing that's very odd. Mrs. Luce had been with her for donkeys' years and Mavis always swore that she would last her out. But only a few days ago she suddenly announced that Mrs. Luce was past it, always making mistakes and refusing to use a word processor, and she was going to get somebody from an agency. That must be the woman you saw. Gosh—is it really half past eleven? I've got to rush."

"Me too," said Paula. "See you. Give me a call."

"I will," promised Annie. "This evening."

Paula got into her car, glad to be sheltered from the wind and the renewed rain, and turned the ignition key. Nothing happened. After five minutes of increasing frustration she resigned herself to the fact that the engine was just not going to start. Much dampness, too many short runs, and a failing battery had temporarily immobilised it.

What a pity she had let Annie go. At least she could have got a lift to the tube station. James had left for work ages ago. She could go home and phone the A.A., but they would be very busy on a morning like this and she would probably have a very long wait.

"Taxi, I suppose," she muttered to herself. "If I can get one to come out here."

She let herself into the house and picked up the telephone in the living-room. The cats had settled down into their morning nap and the whole place seemed to be slumbering.

Paula felt almost like an intruder in her own home, bringing her own little aura of tension and frustration and irritability into the peaceful scene. She tried three phone numbers for taxis and received no response.

After the last failure, she thought for a moment and then dialled Rupert's number. He answered at once. Of course he would be delighted to help. He'd got practically nothing to do and he had still got the use of Mrs. Potts's car.

"If you'll leave me the keys of your mini," he said as they drove away, "I'll try and get it started when I get back."

Paula handed them over, thinking that as she and James had decided that Rupert was not guilty of any serious misdeeds, they might as well act on this belief. Of course they could yet be proved wrong: They had only heard Rupert's version of the story of his life and he might yet turn out to be a first-class con-man. But if that were the case, Paula felt that he would hardly bother with such trivialities as stealing her three-year-old car.

"I was spying on you earlier this morning," she said brightly.

"What?"

He was startled: The white Mercedes swerved very slightly.

"Oh, not on you personally," Paula hastily reassured him. "I'd intended to walk on the Heath, but the wind was so strong that I ended up clinging to your fence, more or less."

Rupert gave a sort of groan. "That fence! Totally inadequate for security. It's the bane of my life."

"Have you ever had any break-ins?"

"Twice I've found somebody in the garden. Teenage boys. They hadn't done any damage. It seemed to be more a question of proving they could get over an obstacle than of housebreaking with evil intent. One of them got quite friendly. It turned out he was playing the trumpet in his school orchestra."

"Well I didn't try any fence-climbing," said Paula, determined to pursue her own subject, "but I did climb an extremely prickly slope and discovered a good view of the back of the house. And while pausing to get my breath back I did wonder which was Mavis's bedroom."

"She sleeps at the front of the house, like Mrs. P.," replied Rupert. "My bed-sitter looks out at the side, over the Heath."

"Ah. I did wonder which was your window, but all I saw was Mavis's office with a desk and a word processor and a secretary. At least I suppose she was a secretary. I'm being nosy," went on Paula, "because I'm very intrigued by Mavis's behaviour, and I'm not the only one. I was talking to Annie just now."

"Annie Lawrence is a pest," said Rupert. "She keeps asking me what's the matter with Mavis, and I don't know. I wish I did."

"She asked me to ask you," said Paula bluntly.

"Damn the woman!"

Again Rupert seemed to be not quite in control of the car as he overtook a couple of slower-moving vehicles.

"Sorry," he said. "My nerves seem to be shot to pieces. Do you mind if we don't talk while I'm driving?"

"*I'm* sorry," said Paula. "Thoughtless of me."

They continued in silence for some minutes, and when they arrived at the Princess Elizabeth College, Paula thanked him and added, "Come and have lunch with me. If you can find anywhere to park this monster. The refectory's not bad—we actually get waited on in one part of it, and James will almost certainly be there."

Rupert seemed to hesitate, glancing down at his jeans and waterproof jacket.

Paula laughed. "They don't dress up, in spite of the waitresses. You're a fashion plate compared with most of the students and staff. Look, there's somebody driving off—you might just get in there."

The refectory was surprisingly peaceful for a school in central London, and Paula and Rupert joined James at a table in a far corner.

"So what have you been doing this morning?" said James, turning to Paula after they had ordered their soup.

Paula ticked it off on her fingers. "Item one, handed one anonymous letter to Sergeant Cox, who promised to look into it. Item two, called on Jill Race with flowers, and spent forty minutes helping Melissa to clean up the house and twenty minutes chatting to Jill. Item three, feeling in need of fresh air, started out to walk for a little while on the Heath but was nearly blown away. Explored round the back of Rupert's place instead, and saw Mavis's secretary at a back window, working away on a word processor. Item four, went to fetch car, got into conversation with Annie, who is working on a book with Mavis and is very worried that Mavis will die or get herself killed before the book is finished. Annie says that Mavis is in a bad way, very scared, not herself at all, that she has sacked her secretary of many years' standing and got an agency girl, and Annie wanted me to find out what the matter was. Here's our soup. I'm starving. Rupert will tell you about item five."

That's put James into the picture, said Paula to herself; he can take over now.

James did take over, most efficiently, and Rupert became noticeably more at ease.

Paula ate and listened. Only once did she intervene. Rupert had explained that Mavis had got Chris to fix the locks of the communicating doors so that there was no access from the other house.

"And it's just as well that I hadn't left anything of mine that I needed over there," he added, "because there's no prospect of getting into my room."

"Do you mind my asking, Rupert," said Paula, "how things stood between you and Chris Williams before Mrs. Potts died? I'm a bit puzzled, because I had the impression that you two were by way of being buddies. In an old-fashioned sense," she added hastily. "Nighttime conspirators."

She spoke without looking at him, and returned with

enthusiasm to her chicken pilaff as soon as she had finished. James was looking surprised, Rupert rather puzzled, when finally she did glance up.

"Who on earth," began Rupert, and then he added: "Oh, it must have been the younger Race girl. I thought I saw her sneaking into the garden. Well, I suppose I'd better come clean. Not that there's anything new to tell, after last evening's confessional. Chris Williams is a dirty little blackmailer. I haven't had any of the poison-pen letters that seem to be going the rounds, but I did get a nasty little note from him saying it would be to my advantage to meet him on the doorstep of Number Eleven at some unearthly hour, followed by a strong suggestion that he knew a lot about my past history."

"And what transpired?" enquired James.

"A neatly phrased suggestion that we should get together to eliminate one or both of the rich old ladies in my charge, with various proposals of how this could be carried out."

"And your response?"

"I prevaricated—told him I didn't go in for that sort of thing, but that I would think about it and decide what to do. He could have taken it that I would eventually agree, or he could have taken it that I was thinking of going to the police. I wish now that I'd told him to go to hell straight away."

"I doubt if it would have made any difference to subsequent events," said James, "but it's yet another reason for bringing it all out into the open. I take it you've kept the note—? Good. Truly, Rupert, I don't think you've got any alternative now. Look, I've got a suggestion. I'm going home after lunch. Suppose I leave my car here for Paula to use later, and you drive me back to Hampstead and we can go to the police station straight away together. What do you think?"

"I've promised to try to get Paula's mini started," said Rupert doubtfully.

James made a very rude remark about Paula's mini, and

Paula, quickly swallowing a mouthful, protested equally forcibly about the condition of James's Renault.

By the time they had finished trading insults, Rupert had come to a decision which was applauded by the other two.

"Ask for Sergeant Cox," said Paula. "He's quite human."

The rest of the meal passed surprisingly cheerfully. Rupert seemed to be making a considerable effort to answer their questions about Mavis.

"I wondered whether Chris had some sort of hold over her too," he said.

"It would have to be something from a long time ago," was James's comment. "After all, what serious indiscretions could one commit at the age of ninety-two?"

"It seems to be Chris's manner of operating, though," said Paula thoughtfully. "Leeching onto his victim with what seems to be a great deal of tender care." She was thinking of Jill. "Quite a subtle kind of torment," she added, getting up from the table. "I've got to go now. I promised to see a couple of Jill's students for her. Good luck to you guys. I'll be home about six."

19

Paula was later than she had expected in getting away from college, and she did not arrive back in Heathview Villas until half-past seven. By this hour it was always difficult to find a parking space, and particularly so for her this evening, as she was driving James's car, which was much bigger than her own.

Rather than waste time searching, she decided to leave the car on the approach road to the Villas, not far from the spot where she had rescued Jill, and walk the rest of the way. James could collect his Renault later.

We shall have to give up some of our front garden, and make a carport, she decided as she lugged her heavy briefcase along; that's one of the drawbacks of buying old property—no garage.

The case seemed to get heavier and heavier as she walked. As she was approaching Gordon's house, Number 3, Paula thought—why not call in now, it will give me a rest and save coming out later.

So she climbed the steps, rested the heavy case on the low stone wall alongside, and rang the bell.

Nobody came. Paula rang again, regretting her decision not to go straight home. She was just about to give up and turn away when the door was opened at last, only a few inches. A very frightened young voice asked, "Who is it?"

"Is that Sylvie?" asked Paula, and quickly explained her errand.

The chain was then removed and the door opened. Sylvie looked distraught, but even with tear-stained face and straggly hair she was still startlingly beautiful.

"Whatever is the matter, child?" cried Paula. "Shall I come in?"

Sylvie gave a loud wail and clutched Paula by the arm. "Oh, I'm so frightened. Gordon's left me to look after her and I'm so afraid he'll get murdered too."

That was what Paula thought the girl said, but Sylvie was so incoherent that it could well have been something else. Eventually, after much coaxing and reassurance, a rather clearer narrative emerged.

Apparently Melissa was upstairs in one of the spare rooms, dead to the world. She had turned up on the doorstep about an hour and a half ago, completely hysterical and screaming blue murder. Yes, honestly.

Sylvie began to recover as she saw Paula's most gratifying response to her story. "It was her mother who'd done it. But it was self-defence. It must have been. I mean, Mel's mother would never kill anybody, would she, unless they went for her first?"

"Sylvie, please, please," begged Paula. "Try to speak more slowly. Who was attacking Melissa's mother?"

"Why, Chris Williams of course. Mel's mother—you know she's got a broken ankle—she was in the kitchen, sitting at the table cutting bread and butter for sandwiches for their supper—she said she was bored and wanted to do something, Mel said—so Mel didn't try to stop her—and Mel had gone upstairs to find something and it took longer than she thought, and she heard somebody come in and she thought it was Carol come home, but it was Chris come in from next door."

Paula exclaimed in horror. "The keys! If only Jill—"

"Mel came running down," continued Sylvie, "and heard Chris and her mother yelling at each other—she was screaming at him to leave her alone, and he was shouting—'You bitch, I'll ruin you,' or something like that. And she was holding the breadknife, and Mel says they sort of struggled, and he sort of fell on the knife, and then she fell and there was a most terrible noise and groaning and screaming and they were both on the floor, and Mel could see blood, and she ran to the phone but couldn't remember any number to call, and then she ran out of the house and came to us. And luckily Gordon came home and he called Dr. Garrett at once and told me to keep Melissa here till she came, and he'd go himself to see what had happened. Would you like some whisky, or brandy or something?"

This offer was made in quite a normal tone of voice. Sylvie seemed to have talked herself into something like calmness.

Paula said she would prefer coffee, and they moved into Gordon's kitchen together. It was very orderly, she noticed, and in spite of her agitation, Sylvie moved with neatness and efficiency. A good housekeeper, Melissa had said; yes, the girl certainly seemed to be that.

"So Dr. Mary Garrett came here to see Melissa," said Paula, sitting down at the kitchen table. Somehow this seemed less heartless than removing to the comfort of the sitting-room.

"She gave her a sedative," explained Sylvie, "and told me to let her sleep as long as she needed. And then she said she'd better go along and see what was happening at Number Ten. She didn't sound very pleased about it."

"And what is happening now? Has Gordon been back?"

"No, but he phoned." Sylvie took a gulp of coffee.

"And—?" said Paula.

Sylvia, now apparently quite recovered, seemed to be taking pleasure in dragging out the story.

"He said the police and the ambulance had arrived, and that they'd taken both Chris and Mel's mum to hospital. Chris wasn't expected to live, but Mrs. Race wasn't so badly hurt. Of course she's got a broken ankle too."

"It isn't broken," said Paula irritably. "Only very badly bruised. What about Carol? Did Gordon say if she'd come home?"

"She wasn't home yet. He was going to wait for her. They were leaving a policewoman to wait for her too and tell her the news. I don't see why Gordon had to wait as well. It's

not as if Carol is at all sensitive, like Melissa is. She hasn't
got much feeling."

Oh, you stupid child, thought Paula, but controlled
herself from saying it out loud.

"I'm sure Gordon will be back as soon as he can," she
said, getting up from the table. "And he'll be wanting a
meal. Why don't you start making it?"

"Yes, I guess I could do that," said Sylvie.

Paula left her to it. She felt slightly guilty as she closed
the front door behind her. After all, the girl was very
distressed, naturally enough. But Gordon would soon be
back to look after her, and Sylvie's troubles were nothing to
what Carol's must be, at this very moment.

James and I must get her out of it, quickly, Paula told herself.
She must stay the night with us. She can have the little room on
the second floor. But first of all she'll want to go to hospital to see
her mother. James will take her. Oh poor Carol, poor Carol.

Her mind full of these plans, she opened her front door and
called out to James. There was no reply. She opened the living-
room door and both kittens shot out, mewing loudly. He must
have left in a great hurry, she thought, not noticing that he had
shut them in. Presumably he was round at Jill's place now.

Paula picked up the telephone and dialled the number.
Nobody answered. Perhaps she had pressed the wrong buttons.
She tried again with the same result. What was happening,
where were they all? Had Sylvie been making it all up, this
horror in Jill's house that Paula now felt had been just waiting
to happen, that she herself ought somehow to have prevented?

She got up to fetch her cigarettes, which she had left in
her briefcase, now lying on the table in the hall. As she did
so, she noticed that there was a slip of paper taped to the
bottom of the mirror in the hall. In her haste and anxiety she
had failed to see it before.

Only yesterday she and James had decided that this was
the best place to leave messages for each other, since it was
outside the reach of the climbing kittens. The hall table,
where they had previously left such messages, was now one
of the favourite leaping spots.

Feeling comforted and reassured, Paula read the message. "I'm driving Carol to the hospital to see her mother—in shock after a fight with Chris, who was seriously hurt. Rupert will tell you about it. In great haste, love, J."

Underneath, in an even more hurried scrawl, was written, "Cats not fed."

Paula placed the note back on the mirror, and went on into the kitchen, feeling some relief at knowing that Sylvie's fantastic story really was true, and even greater relief that James was doing what she herself would have wanted.

Sally and Sam were climbing over everything hunting for something to eat. Paula retrieved them from the top of the cooker and the windowsill behind the sink respectively, and placed them firmly on the floor beside their bowls, into which she hurriedly poured dried food from a packet kept in a closed cupboard.

Then she filled another bowl with milk and sat down at the kitchen table to watch the kittens' tails waving and listen to the contented crunching. After a few minutes she felt considerably less agitated, and she got up to telephone Rupert.

"Oh Paula, I've been expecting you," was his eager greeting, but immediately afterwards his words were drowned by the sound of loud barking.

"Shut up, Bessie!" yelled Rupert. "Sorry, Paula," he added, "it's Gordon's dogs. Hold on a minute. I'll try and shut them in the kitchen and use the phone in the hall."

Paula waited. The sounds coming over the wire indicated that he was having considerable difficulty. When at last his voice came again she said, "Don't rush it, Rupert. Get your breath back, and then tell me. Slowly. Why on earth have you got Gordon's dogs?"

Rupert groaned. "I wish I knew. I'd come out to see what all the commotion was about—police cars, ambulance, the lot—and there was Gordon turning his car round in our drive, and he got out, and out shot the dogs—damn silly car to have when you've got Alsatians, you need something bigger, with a hatchback—and he put their leads into my hands and said something like, 'Hang on to them for a sec, would you, while I rearrange this stuff I've got in the back.' "

"So you did hang on to them?"

"Wouldn't you? He'd let go of the leads and I couldn't have them rampaging around the garden."

"Actually I believe they're very well trained," said Paula.

"Not with me they aren't. Anyway, there I stood like the world's prize idiot while he just drove away and hasn't been seen or heard of since."

"You've tried his house?"

"With considerable difficulty I managed to phone. I only got Sylvie in hysterics, wanting to know when Gordon was coming back. She wasn't in the least bit interested in the dogs."

"When did this happen?" Paula asked.

Rupert groaned again. "It feels like hours. Paula, do you think you could come round here? James called just before he left for the hospital with Carol and asked me to bring you up to date with events. He was very sorry about the dogs and promised to help when he got back, but meanwhile—" He broke off, swore softly, and then asked, "Unless I can bring them round to your place?"

"No way," cried Paula vehemently. "The cats would hate it."

"Sorry. I'd forgotten."

"I'll be with you in ten minutes."

Paula fought back a tendency to hysterical laughter as she put down the phone. She wrote the words, "I'm at Rupert's," underneath the message that James had left for her, replaced it on the hall mirror, and left the house.

As she walked the few yards to the far end of Heathview Villas she remembered how anxiously Sylvie had been awaiting Gordon's return. Presumably he was not intending to return; not yet, at any rate. Had he dumped the dogs on Rupert while he carried out some errand, or could he perhaps be doing a disappearing act, and if so, why?

Perhaps Rupert would know more. In any case it was a great comfort to have someone to talk to instead of all this solitary worrying and speculating.

20

"I've given them half the contents of the fridge," said Rupert when he opened the door to Paula, "and two of the best blankets from the laundry cupboard, and they're settled down in the utility room by the back door, so I think we might get a little peace. Let's go to my room."

Paula followed him upstairs. It was natural, she supposed, that his mind should still be full of his own dilemma, but she hoped to get him off the subject of the Alsatians for long enough to bring her up to date with the evening's happenings. She was also beginning to feel hungry. The lunch in the college refectory had been a long time ago. It would have been sensible to get something to eat for herself when she fed the cats, but it was too late now.

Rupert pushed open the door of the bed-sittingroom.

"I was eating a sandwich when you phoned," he said. "I thought you'd like one too. Sorry it's only rather stale cheese."

Paula was effusive in her thanks. "How many people would have thought of that," she added. "Rupert, you've got to get out of this bad patch in your life and into a worthwhile job. Tell me about yourself first. Did you make your confession?"

"James made me stick to it," he replied ruefully. "I'd have chickened out if it hadn't been for him."

"And what happened?"

"Sergeant Cox noted it down, but I don't think he was very impressed. I've not actually committed any crime other than faking references, and they're certainly not going to waste time on that. It's up to Mrs. Potts's lawyers to take action against me if they want to."

"Gordon's firm?"

"That's right. But I've a feeling they won't."

"Oh? Why not?"

"Because they've got their own problems at the moment. One of the partners has been dipping his hands in the till."

"I knew it, I knew it!" cried Paula excitedly. "I've thought all along there was something crooked about Gordon. Was it him? And how do you know?"

"I only found out this afternoon, after James and I had been to the police and before all the racket started. I know one of the guys in the office quite well. I actually told him I'd got this job under false pretenses—once you start confessing it seems to become a habit—and he wasn't the least bit concerned. He thought it was Mrs. Potts's money they'd been speculating with. It might have been Gordon—he wouldn't mention any names. I won't bother you with the details—frankly I don't really understand them myself. I've no head for that sort of fraud. Petty crime—that's my style."

"Not from now on it isn't," said Paula firmly. "Do I take it that even if they knew you'd forged the references they wouldn't bother to do anything about it now?"

"That's about it. Aren't I lucky? Virtue is its own reward. But I'm rather sorry now that I told the police. Have this last sandwich. I don't want any more."

Paula thanked him and helped herself. "I think it's a good thing you made your confession," she said. "You've covered yourself all round, and the police won't do anything unless somebody asks them to. Didn't James think so?"

"James doesn't yet know about this last development," said Rupert. "That was after he got caught up in the fracas at Number Ten. We didn't get much chance to talk again. Oh, by the way, I got your car started, but you really need to run it around a bit."

"Not tonight. Tomorrow. Thanks, anyway. Now please tell me what has happened to Jill and Chris. I had the most garbled version from Sylvie and am rather confused."

"I'm afraid I'm not much wiser. James couldn't stop to tell me in detail, but I'll do my best."

Rupert, with his mind temporarily at ease about the Alsatians, clearly was doing his best, but Paula found his story scarcely more helpful than Sylvie's had been.

"But who started it?" she asked. "That's what I want to know. Did Chris actually try to grab the breadknife, or did Jill go for him first?"

"I don't know," replied Rupert. "The only person who could possibly know is Melissa, but she's not in a position to be questioned, and she probably won't be able to help even when she is."

"But the injuries—"

"Chris got a stab wound in the chest. They were going to operate, but the ambulance men didn't think he'd got much chance."

"So that must have been Jill's doing. What does Jill say?"

"Nothing intelligible. She's in a state of shock. She's got a cut on her arm, I believe. Not very deep. At one point he'd obviously managed to turn the knife round on her."

"And what happened next?"

"Melissa ran off to Gordon—you know about that. Gordon called the police and ambulance, and I think James came out to see what was happening, and made a statement to the police. So did Gordon, of course. I think at that moment the main concern was for Carol, poor kid. They'd checked that Melissa had been attended to. Dr. Mary Garrett told them about that."

"So did you actually see James?"

"No. He phoned. That was before Gordon came and dumped the dogs on me. Or was it?" Rupert put both hands to his forehead and made a grimace. "Paula, I'm awfully sorry. I'm getting muddled myself. Sometime in all this melee Annie came along to fetch Mavis. I assumed that Mavis had called her to come and collect her. She still doesn't communicate with me, of course."

He paused, and Paula waited patiently, grateful that she had not got the job of sifting the evidence, but was only trying to satisfy her own curiosity.

"No, wait a minute, I've got it straight," said Rupert at last. "James phoned. Then I came out into the front garden, sort of vaguely hoping that I could talk to him, and I saw Annie helping Mavis into her car. It's only a little 'un, like yours. She doesn't use our drive to turn round in, as some people do."

"Gordon," prompted Paula.

"That's right. He'd been parked farther along the road. The dogs must have been in the car all the time."

"Sylvie says he'd just got home when Melissa came rushing to them for help. Had he already got the dogs in the car and not yet let them out? Or did he deliberately take the dogs when he came along to see what had happened, and if so, why?"

"Those bloody Alsatians," said Rupert. "I'm sure they're the clue to something." He got up from his chair. "Sorry, Paula, I'll have to go and see. They're barking again."

"Just a minute." Paula stood up too. "I've got an idea. Gordon's wife—do you know her, Rupert?"

"I've seen her. She's rather gorgeous. Can't say I actually know her, no. She doesn't mix with the likes of me. The hired help."

"Melissa knows her. And Sylvie visits her regularly. And the dogs were originally hers. So I'm told. So why don't you take them along to Sylvie and get her to get Gordon's wife to deal with them? Don't you think that's the answer? Honestly, Rupert," went on Paula as he did not immediately respond, "you're no use to yourself or to anybody else—

you're only one-quarter with us as long as you're worrying about those animals."

"You've said it!"

Rupert sprang into life, grabbed Paula by the arm, and rushed her downstairs and along the passage to the back of the house. There he flung open a door and cried, "Look out! The monsters are friendly."

Paula, though fond of animals, found herself over-whelmed. Rupert, who suddenly looked about fifteen years younger, was playing with the dogs, wrestling with them, rather to Paula's alarm.

"Had we better phone Sylvie first?" he asked when matters were rather more under control.

"No," said Paula firmly. "We're only taking them home."

"Do you want me to get the car out?"

"For five minutes' walk?"

"Sorry. It's all this living with ancient ladies."

"It won't be for much longer. Come on—what's your name—Mitzi? What a silly name for a creature this size."

The short walk was uneventful, although Paula had the feeling that they were being stared at from behind closed windows, and Rupert's sudden cheerfulness was almost oppressive.

Sylvie came to the door, stared at Paula and Rupert and the dogs as if she had never seen any of them before, and said: "Oh, what do you want?"

"We've brought Bessie and Mitzi home," said Rupert. "Aren't you going to take them?"

"Oh," said Sylvie again. "Wait a minute."

They moved forward expectantly, but she shut the door on them.

After a stunned second Rupert did a little dance on the doorstep, playing with Bessie.

"They've done it again," he shouted. "Dumped the dogs on me."

"Oh shut up," said Paula irritably. "They can't do that to us." She put her finger on the bell and held it there.

After about half a minute the door was opened again. A woman of about Paula's age stood there. She was very tall and thin, and very fair. She smiled with an air of great disdain and spoke very coldly.

"I must apologise for my stepdaughter's behaviour. The events of this evening have rather upset her. Down, Bessie, down Mitzi!"

The Alsatians, who had been straining to get at her, responded with grovelling meekness. Rupert handed over their leads.

"Thank you for looking after them," said the woman. "I'm sorry you were troubled."

She would have shut the door again then, but Rupert stepped forward and held it open. "Like a bloody salesman," he said to Paula afterwards.

"Are you Sylvia Vincent?" he asked abruptly.

"I am," she replied with a slight raise of the eyebrows and in an even colder voice.

"Then perhaps you would be kind enough to convey a message to your husband—your former husband, I beg your pardon—"

Paula tugged warningly at Rupert's arm.

"Oh, all right," he said ungraciously, "but I'd like to say what I think of him."

Sylvia Vincent smiled. At least Paula thought it was a smile, and when she spoke it sounded as if she were genuinely amused.

"I assure you there is no need to. You are not alone in your opinion. Thank you again. Goodnight."

Once more the door closed, and Rupert made no objection when Paula dragged him away.

At the front gate, however, he paused and said, "I ought to have told her that they'd been fed."

"She'll find that out for herself," said Paula. "Come on, let's get out of here."

"What did you think of her?"

Paula's reply was interrupted by Sylvie, who had come

out of the house and run after them and was speaking even
more breathlessly than usual. "Please—please don't mind
Sylvia, she doesn't mean to be bitchy, she's awfully grateful
really. She's going to stay with me—me and Melissa—till
Gordon comes back. Please, you mustn't mind her."

Paula stopped to reassure her, but Rupert now seemed
anxious to get away.

"You go on if you like," said Paula. "I want to speak to
Sylvie."

Rupert muttered something about wanting to get home,
and he moved about restlessly, but still within earshot.

"Sylvie," said Paula, "do you think Gordon is going to
come back at all?"

The straightforward question seemed to steady the girl.
"We don't know," she replied quite calmly. "Sylvia thinks
he probably won't."

"Do you know why?"

"Well, he's been threatening to go and join this woman in
Sri Lanka, but Sylvia thinks he'd be terribly bored, living
there all the time."

Woman in Sri Lanka, Paula said to herself; that must be
the regular one. Aloud she said, "Please could you try and
remember, Sylvie, how he seemed when he came home this
evening. Did you get the impression that he was not going
to stay home?"

"I'm awfully sorry," said Sylvie, "I just can't remember
how he was at all. You see, Mel had just turned up in an
awful state, and I was so glad to see Gordon that I just
grabbed him and asked him to help."

"I quite understand," said Paula. "But surely you would
notice if he had got the dogs with him?"

"Oh yes, he'd got the dogs in the car. He'd been home
earlier and collected them to run them on the Heath. He
always takes them over to the other side for their run."

"So he'd already been home once. How did he seem
then?"

"Just as usual," said Sylvie. "Please, do you mind if I go?

Sylvia didn't want me to come and talk to you—she hates people talking about him."

"I'm sorry," said Paula, feeling a sudden and quite unexpected surge of sympathy for Gordon's former wife. "Thanks for coming."

Sylvie ran back to the house, but she had only got halfway along the garden path when she turned again and cried out to Paula, who had already joined Rupert outside the front gate.

"Sorry, I'd forgotten," she gasped. "When I was telling Gordon about Mel he picked up something from the front doormat. I didn't see it properly—I wasn't thinking about it—Mel was screaming away behind me—but I'm sure Gordon picked up something."

"An envelope—a piece of paper?" suggested Paula.

"Yes, I think so. I think it was an envelope. I suppose it was addressed to him. I think—yes, I'm sure—he put it in his jacket pocket. Does that help?"

Paula thanked her, but she was already back on the doorstep.

"Did you hear that?" Paula turned to Rupert. "Somebody had sent Gordon a letter, presumably delivered by hand, between the time he came home and collected the dogs and the time he returned with them before rushing off to Jill's house."

"Yes, I heard," said Rupert.

"Now if we could find out who it was and what was in the letter," began Paula.

"Just how do you propose to do that?"

He sounded tired and irritable. These sudden changes of mood are disconcerting, thought Paula: James seems to cope with them better than I can.

She made a noncommittal reply, and they walked the next few yards in silence, but when they came opposite her house she said, "Oh, good. There's a light on upstairs. James must be home. Do you want to come in, Rupert?"

"No, thanks." He seemed to be trying to make an effort to

be more amiable. "You'll want to talk to James and I think I've had enough for one day. Thank you both for everything. I don't see how I can possibly repay you."

"There's no need," began Paula, but he had already walked away.

For a moment or two she stood looking after him, puzzled and disturbed. Was it possible that she and James were both wrong about Rupert? They were taking his word for so much; they hadn't heard any other opinions of him—only Mavis's sudden intense antipathy, which they had been attributing to the eccentricities of a very old lady novelist. They had never actually talked about Rupert to anybody else. Except—yes. A recent memory returned suddenly.

Gordon's party, when they had been introduced to other residents of Heathview Villas. Gordon had talked about Rupert. "He's the most private and mysterious of us all," Gordon had said, or something along those lines.

But how far could one trust Gordon in anything, either personally or professionally? Not at all, decided Paula, feeling ashamed that she had ever been attracted to him. Sylvia Vincent's feelings were plain enough; for all Paula knew, Sylvia was only the last of a series of ex-wives. Not to mention the lady in Sri Lanka. And as for the professional side, well, she felt very inclined to believe Rupert's version of that until it was proved false.

One has to trust somebody sometimes, she thought as she let herself into the house, and added in her mind a little prayer of thankfulness that at any rate there was one man she could trust thoroughly, in every way and at all times.

But it hasn't always been like that with James, she mentally corrected herself, as memories from past years suddenly surfaced in her consciousness, as is the way of memories.

21

James was not alone.

He and Carol were sitting in the living-room, deep in conversation. Paula was surprised, even a little disappointed, until she remembered that this was in fact what she had been hoping for, that Carol would take refuge with James and herself. The switchover from wanting reassurance herself to being the one who did the comforting was made in a flash, barely consciously but not entirely successfully.

"How is your mother, Carol?" she asked.

The girl looked very tired, but quite calm.

"She's resting," she replied. "The police said they wouldn't ask her any more questions tonight. They said at the hospital that she can come home in the morning."

"And what about you?" Paula looked first at Carol and then at James as she spoke.

"I'm trying to persuade her to stay with us," he said, "but she swears she'll be all right on her own."

"I do appreciate it," said Carol formally, "and it's great to know that you're here, but—I know it sounds crazy—but I'd rather be alone. Just for tonight. Before Mother and Mel come and take over again tomorrow."

"Oh I do understand," said Paula with a warmth that was now completely sincere. "I know how you feel. At least I think I do. You know that Melissa is with Sylvie, don't you, Carol?"

"Yes. Apparently she's still asleep. Sylvia Vincent told me when I phoned them just now."

"Sylvia Vincent seems to have taken charge of everything, including the dogs," said Paula.

"Dogs?" echoed James and Carol in unison, and then James added, "Oh yes. I'd forgotten. Poor Rupert. What happened?"

Paula was quite happy to tell the story. It brought something like light relief after the shock of events in Carol's home. After they had laughed a little at Rupert's predicament, Carol stood up: "I'll go home now. I want to clean up the kitchen. It's rather disgusting."

"And Melissa and I worked so hard on it this morning," said Paula rather plaintively.

The other two laughed again, and Paula added: "Sorry. Didn't the police clean up? They usually do."

"They mopped up the worst of the blood," said Carol in her most matter-of-fact manner, "but I shan't feel happy until I've scrubbed the floor and the table myself. Don't worry about me. I'll be better for doing something. I'm not that sort of tired. Goodnight and thanks a lot."

After she had gone, Paula said, "I don't like it, Carol being there alone."

"Neither do I," said James, "but she's made up her mind."

"I'm thinking of those keys," said Paula. "Jill said this morning that she'd have to get the locks changed because Chris wouldn't give up the keys—where would they be now, James?"

"You mean Chris had Jill's front door keys?"

"Not her own. A spare set."

"Ah!" James drew a breath of comprehension. "That explains it. That's how he got in. We couldn't make sense of it. Obviously Jill hadn't let him in, and we thought it had to be Melissa, but since she wasn't available for questioning—"

"When you say 'we' you mean—"

"Sergeant Cox and his constable and the police surgeon and the ambulance men and Gordon and whoever else happened to be around."

"How did *you* get involved, darling?"

"Oh, that was Gordon. He'd parked outside our gate, and I was in the front garden rescuing Sally. She'd climbed up the cherry tree and got stuck—and we really must try of stop them getting round to the front of the house. I don't want them in the road."

"I know," said Paula. "It's usually Sally. Why is the female the more adventurous one?"

"You tell me. I wouldn't know. Anyway, Gordon called out that there'd been a death at Jill's and I said I'd come and help. And you know what we found."

"James—when Gordon got out of his car, did you notice if the dogs were in the back?"

"Rupert says so," began James slowly, and then added: "Yes, of course they were. I was outside the gate, hanging on to Sally, who wasn't the least bit grateful for being rescued and was clawing at me. She noticed the dogs. She was getting ready to fight, and they started barking."

"And afterwards, when you'd called the police and ambulance and they'd moved the casualties and you'd made your statements—how did Gordon behave?"

"Oh, for heaven's sake, Paula, we'd got one person nearly dead and another either in shock or hysterical or both. How do you think Gordon behaved? How d'you think I behaved? We got help at once and tried to explain what had happened. We weren't interested in subtleties. What are you driving at, anyway?"

Hastily Paula explained about the envelope that Sylvie had seen Gordon pick up.

"That could be what decided him to quit," she concluded. "And I was wondering whether he'd already read it when he met you, or whether he only looked at it afterwards, while you were waiting for the ambulance perhaps."

James subsided. "Yes, he could have done. It rather turned our stomachs, both of us, but we were having a sort of unspoken competition at appearing to be tough, pretending we wanted to use the bathroom in any case. But don't ask me whether I noticed any change in his behaviour, because I didn't."

"He's not a guy to show what he's really thinking," said Paula, "but at least this is beginning to make sense. And now let's talk about something more cheerful. I wish I'd seen Sally up the tree, the little devil. How far had she got?"

The kittens are our code language, thought Paula, as James allowed his spurt of temper to subside; to talk of them shows a will for peace and harmony. But a little later he returned voluntarily to the subject of the scene at Jill's house.

"You were right about Chris Williams blackmailing her. And it wasn't about that footling tax fiddle."

Paula, who had almost fallen asleep in her armchair, and was wondering how to get up the energy to go to bed, was instantly alert.

"Carol thinks she's got to the root of it," went on James. "She says her mother has never stopped hoping that her husband will come back, that he'll get tired of ministering to his wealthy old lady and as he gets older himself he'll want his adoring wife to run round after him. Carol thinks it's not impossible, provided he never finds out what Jill did to try to stop him leaving in the first place."

"Ah," said Paula, "now we're getting somewhere. What did Jill do?"

"Wrote a letter to the other woman explaining what a bastard he—Jill's husband—was, and going into the sort of detail that one just doesn't say, let alone put into words on paper. If that ever came into the hands of Jill's husband—whose name, by the way, is Patrick—any chance of their getting together again would be nil."

"Poor Jill," said Paula. "Yes, I can imagine her doing that. You leave my man alone, he's a stinker, but he's mine.

Presumably she thought it would put the lady off him, which it didn't. And presumably the lady had the sense not to show it to him. But how did Chris come into it?"

"Apparently she's quite well known in the art world, writes a bit of criticism, collects a bit. She knew Bertie Revelson and visited him. That's how Jill and Patrick got to know her. Maybe she got friendly with Chris. Did she actually give him the letter? Did he steal it? We shall never know, but he seems to have got hold of it somehow. A nice little addition to his blackmailing files."

"But James," protested Paula, "he couldn't get much money out of Jill."

"In her case it was probably a matter of tormenting the victim."

"And now she's rid of him."

For a little while they were both silent and thoughtful. Then Paula said, "I suppose she *is* rid of him?"

"Yes. He died before Carol and I left the hospital."

"Will she be charged with murder?"

"If anything," said James, "it will be self-defence. They both had hold of the knife. There's no means of proving anything except that there was a struggle. What Carol is mainly concerned about is her mother's state of mind. And, of course, the whereabouts of that letter."

"Would Chris have had it on him?"

"The big question," said James.

Again there was a silence.

"There's a sister who is next-of-kin," said James presently. "She will no doubt dispose of his possessions. And Revelson's daughter is supposed to be coming shortly to deal with the house."

"If only we could get in first and find the blackmail hoard," exclaimed Paula.

James laughed. "Who knows? Somebody else might have the same idea. I hope you're not thinking of housebreaking. I'm all for helping the girls as much as we can, but there is a limit."

Paula agreed, and then suggested, only half seriously, that they could at least keep watch on Number 11 next door to see if anybody tried to get in.

"You can do what you like," said James. "I'm going to bed. Damn. Who's calling at this hour?"

Paula reached for the phone; a woman's voice she didn't recognise came on the line.

"I'm awfully sorry to disturb you, but I'm worried about Mavis. Have you seen her?"

"Have I seen Mavis?" repeated Paula in bewilderment. "Oh, is this Annie?"

"Yes. Sorry. Obviously you haven't. Sorry again."

"Hi—don't ring off. What's happened, Annie?"

Paula made a sign to James to pick up another extension, and after a slight hesitation he moved out into the hall.

"She asked me to come and fetch her when all the drama started," said Annie. "Which I did. It was hellishly inconvenient, with two of the kids having flu, and Derek in a foul temper, but I've got to keep Mavis functioning somehow until we've finished the book."

"That must have been hours ago," remarked Paula.

"It sure was. It feels like centuries. She wouldn't do any work—admittedly I wasn't exactly in the mood for it myself—and we put her in the little sitting-room with the television and tried to keep the kids out of the way, but she wouldn't stay there, and kept following me around and moaning."

Annie paused.

"Do you mean just sighing wordlessly," said Paula, "or was she actually moaning about something?"

"Sorry, I'm not quite compos mentis myself at the moment. Yes, I mean moaning about something. She kept saying, 'I didn't mean them to die, I never meant it.' Something along those lines. Derek got fed up with it and asked her what the hell did she think she was talking about, which got me worried because I didn't want to offend her, but she took it very quietly and apologised to him and said that of course he wouldn't know, but normally she was always on her own when she was planning the end of a story, and she would wander round the house talking to herself, and that sometimes she found herself killing off characters that she didn't really want to."

Annie paused again.

"Did you and Derek believe this?" asked Paula. "That she was talking about her fictional characters?"

"Well yes, we did. What else could she mean? Can you see Mavis, at her age and with her arthritis, actually going about murdering people?"

"It does seem terribly unlikely," agreed Paula. "But supposing she didn't mean she'd actually killed anyone herself, but had done something that could have led to somebody else doing it. Anyway," she went on hurriedly since Annie did not seem to be responding very sympathetically to this suggestion, "the main thing is, where is she? What actually happened? Didn't you drive her home?"

"Of course I did. Ages ago. But when we got halfway there—more or less opposite Bertie's house—she told me to stop and she'd get out and walk the rest. She needed some fresh air, she said, and she didn't want me to walk with her, and she didn't want me to stay and watch her, and she was going to wait until I'd turned the car round and driven away before she walked on."

"So you did just that?"

"Right first time. But of course I was worried and I phoned several times to check that she'd got home safely, but no reply. And eventually I tried Rupert, and he said he was sorry, but he'd no means of getting into Mavis's house now, but he'd walk round outside and see what lights were on, which he did, and there weren't any. So I asked him if he couldn't break in somehow, and he said he was damned if he would, she'd more or less chucked him out and he didn't care what happened to the old cow. And since then I've been calling round everybody in the Villas and nobody's seen her."

"Maybe she's in bed asleep," suggested Paula. "Or just not answering the phone."

"Maybe," snapped Annie. "Anyway, thanks for listening. Sorry you've been troubled."

And she cut off the call before Paula had a chance to respond.

22

"What on earth did you make of that?"

Paula and James were once more sitting in the big room, staring at each other. It was well past midnight, but they had lost all sense of tiredness.

"I'm going to get hold of Rupert," said James, picking up the phone. "He must have some means of finding out if she's in."

"He's in a foul mood."

"I don't care." James spoke into the receiver. "Rupert, James here. Listen, this is important."

Paula got up and picked up the telephone in the hall.

Rupert's voice sounded surprisingly amiable. "Yes, of course I've got ways of finding out," he was saying, "but I wasn't having that bitch Annie telling me what to do. I haven't looked after all the security arrangements for these two houses for nothing, James, but I'm not going to tell you how—not even you. Anyway, Mavis isn't there. I've been all over the place, looked into every nook and cranny. I'm glad you called. I was just wondering about calling the police."

"Hold it a moment," said James. "Paula's on the other extension. She's trying to tell me something."

Paula had come in from the hall and was tugging at James's sleeve.

"It's a wild idea," she said softly, "but I can't get it out of my mind. Chris's blackmail files. Chris has been tenderly caring for Mavis since Mrs. Potts died. Was it caring? Mavis will know all about what's been going on today. She's been at Annie's, and Annie knows it all."

"You mean Mavis could be trying to get at Chris's papers?"

"Just that."

"Not such a wild idea. How would she get into the house?"

"How are *we* going to?" countered Paula. "Ask Rupert. He's the expert."

James spoke into the phone. Then he put it down and said: "He'll be round in a few minutes. What do you think, Paula, are we wise to trust Rupert as much as we do?"

"That's what I was wondering this afternoon. And yet—"

"I know. Maybe it's my own pride. I just don't want to be wrong about him."

"Let's take comfort from the thought that we are about to commit a felony ourselves," said Paula encouragingly.

Ten minutes later they were all three walking, they hoped unobserved, round to the back entrance of the Revelson house.

This is where I came in, thought Paula; this is where it all started, with Jill dragging me round to call on Bertie and talk about our poison-pen letters. On that occasion they had found the door unlocked. Rupert was examining the door now.

"Any problem?" asked James.

"Not for us. Somebody's already forced it. Come and look."

Paula and James did so.

"That couldn't have been Mavis," said Paula. "She wouldn't have the strength."

To herself she was saying, who did this—Rupert himself? Is this his second visit here tonight? James came closer to her and she felt for his hand.

"Well, what do you want to do?" asked Rupert. "Shall we go in?"

"Of course," said James.

The lights in the kitchen quarters were all on. Just like last time, thought Paula. They looked at the great period piece of a kitchen and at the small well-equipped one next door. Everything seemed to be in perfect order.

"Where would Chris keep his own belongings?" asked James.

"Bedroom?" hazarded Rupert, and added, "I've never been upstairs in this house. Have you?"

"I've never been in this house at all," said James. "Paula?"

"Not upstairs. But I wonder—"

Paula had reached the door that opened into the front hall. James pulled her back. "Let's all go together. There might be someone here."

"I thought of the dining-room," she muttered. "Where Jill and I sat and waited. The drinks-cabinet. There's a large drawer at the bottom, and Chris accused Jill of taking Bertie's will out of it, so maybe it means something to him."

The lights were on in the front hall and on the staircase, but the house was very quiet. Like last time, thought Paula. For a moment they all stood quite still, listening.

Rupert made the first move. "Let's get on with it."

The door of the dining-room was ajar. Rupert pushed it open, stepped into the room, seemed to recoil, and then moved forward again and called out in a voice that was not quite steady.

"Prepare yourselves. Here's another corpse for you."

Mavis was lying on the carpet next to the cabinet, face upwards, eyes closed, mouth open, dark blue coat spread out around her, and lying across the body, with its handle crooked grotesquely around her neck, was the walnut walking stick that she always carried.

"Is it a heart attack?" asked Paula hopefully, coming forward.

"Could be," said Rupert, "but it didn't come naturally."

"You're right," said James.

They all bent closer, Paula gripping Rupert's arm tightly, more to steady him than to calm herself, for she felt almost unnaturally calm, as if she had known all along that they would find something like this.

"She's been hit on the temple, just there," she said. "Can you see where the skin's broken?"

"And the position of the stick " said James. "It couldn't possibly have fallen like that if she'd suddenly collapsed."

Rupert straightened up. "Okay, folks, let's call the police."

"Just a minute," said Paula, walking carefully round Mavis's body so that she could look more closely at the drinks-cabinet. The drawer at the bottom had been pulled right out, and its contents were spilling out onto the carpet.

"Paula!" shouted James. "For Christ's sake don't start—"

"I'm not going to move anything," she interrupted. "I just want to see if—I just want to look for a moment, and we won't get another chance."

James subsided. "Well as long as you don't actually touch."

Paula knelt down on the carpet and peered at the scattered papers. Most of them seemed to be letters, many of which were in handwriting, but they were all muddled up together, and some of the pages had even been crumpled up by whoever had been searching through them. By craning her neck this way and that, she could get tantalising glimpses of bits of writing.

"Now look here, this has got to stop," said James.

Paula did not reply, but Rupert knelt down beside her and she could sense the tension in him.

"Can you see anything about me?" he whispered.

It was at this moment that Paula finally decided that Rupert had been honest with them. All lingering suspicion that he might be playing some game of his own vanished in the certainty that he too had been a victim of Chris's hoarding of blackmailing material, and that he had not known what they were going to find in this house tonight.

"What would it be?" she whispered back.

"I don't know. Legal document of sorts, photocopy perhaps, but how on earth he could have—"

"Would you two *please*," began James, and then suddenly his tone changed: "What's that?"

They had all heard the sound, footsteps perhaps?

"Come on, Rupert," said James. "We'll have to investigate. You keep guard here, Paula, and don't you dare—"

"I won't try to tackle anybody," she said very innocently.

He made an exasperated sound, and the moment they had gone she crouched down on the carpet and stretched out her hand towards some sheets of paper covered with large untidy handwriting. The sheets went into her left-hand jacket pocket, and she began to look around again.

When the others returned a few minutes later she was sitting on one of the armchairs near to the fireplace, staring at Mavis's body with a pitying expression on her face.

"So Mavis was a blackmail victim too," she said. "Presumably that's why she came here, when she heard that Chris was dead. Well, you two? Any luck?"

"They got away, whoever it was," said James. "The back of this house is like a rabbit warren. You've not heard or seen anything, have you?"

"Not a thing," said Paula.

James glanced at her suspiciously, and Paula smiled back.

"I'm calling the police," he snapped, and went out into the hall.

Paula stood up and beckoned to Rupert. When he came closer she put a finger to her lips warningly, and with the other hand transferred something from the right-hand jacket pocket into his.

Then she whispered, "If they search us we'll both be in trouble."

He smiled broadly, lifted her off her feet and swung her around.

When James returned to the room after making his phone call they both looked guilty and slightly out of breath. He stared at them gloomily but made no comment.

"Did you get Sergeant Cox?" asked Paula.

"Yes. And his Inspector. They won't be long."

"Do you think we might have a drink?" Rupert was standing near the cabinet. "After all, we've had a nasty shock."

James looked as if he would like to disapprove, but was very tempted.

"Why not?" he said, taking a step towards Rupert. And then, as the clangour of the ancient front doorbell filled the house, he added, "They can't possibly have got here already."

Paula ran to open the front door, since both the others were slow in making a move.

The girl who stood on the doorstep was shaking and gasping for breath.

"Carol!" cried Paula. "Are you all right?"

"He got away," she said. "I lost him."

"Come and tell us. Take your time. Oh—just a minute."

At the door of the dining-room Paula stopped suddenly.

"It's all right," said Carol, going into the room. "I know what's there. I've seen her. Yes please," she said to Rupert, who had picked up a bottle. "I'd like some gin."

It didn't take her long to recover enough to tell her story, and she managed to give them the gist of it before the police arrived. She had come to search for her mother's letter among Chris's papers, found that the back door had been forced open, come into the house, heard nobody, found Mavis dead, and was about to search among the scattered papers when she heard people moving about.

"That was you," she said. "I thought I'd better hide. I went into the picture gallery and got down behind the settee. When you were all in here I heard someone come downstairs and go out the back, and I followed. And he went out the back door and round into the road and down to the end and along the passageway onto the Heath, and that's when I lost him. I'd no idea which way he'd gone, and I couldn't chase him any longer."

She took a sip from her glass and suddenly leaned back in her chair looking completely exhausted.

"But who was it? Who was it, Carol?"

They were all questioning her at once.

She opened her eyes and looked up in surprise at three eager faces.

"Gordon Vincent, of course," she said, and shut her eyes again.

23

The period that followed was alternately tedious and worrying, but for Paula the memory that remained most vividly in her mind was that of fighting the urgent desire to put her hand into the left-hand pocket of her old green corduroy jacket and check that the pages she had picked up were still there.

Stop it, she kept telling herself angrily: The last thing you want to do is to call attention to it. She wondered if Rupert felt the same. She looked across at him as they were sitting wearily waiting in the big room to tell the police all they could, but Rupert seemed to have undergone one of his rapid mood swings, and was silent and morose.

James was slightly more lively. He was talking to Carol, who had somewhat recovered and was explaining how she had come to the resolution to search Chris's possessions before they were taken away.

"But I never got a chance to look," she concluded, "because you people turned up."

"It's just as well we did," said James. "You could get into quite serious trouble if you tamper with the evidence in a murder case."

He glanced at Paula as he spoke, but she was looking the other way, asking Rupert if he had a cigarette.

"I didn't care about that," said Carol, "I only wanted that letter."

Good girl, thought Paula, and wished she could set her mind at rest at once. But I'll try to get it to her tonight, she mentally added.

"What will happen to all that stuff Chris had collected?" Carol was now asking.

"Presumably it will be handed over to his next-of-kin," replied James.

"His sister, I've seen her," said Carol. "She looked very sour and uptight, but maybe if I explained to her . . ."

Paula got up and moved about the room. Her longing to stop Carol from worrying was overwhelming, but she did not dare risk a confrontation with James, particularly at this moment when the police were in the room across the hall.

"What do you think Mavis could have been looking for?" she said when she sat down again.

Rupert answered: "I can imagine Mavis committing absolutely any indiscretion, but I can't see her caring in the least about who knew it."

"So why was she here?"

"It sounds incredible," Rupert replied, "but I'm wondering if it couldn't have been pure altruism. Suppose she knew she hadn't long to live—why not perform a public service by releasing Chris's victims?"

James scoffed at this suggestion, and an argument threatened. We are all tired and irritable, thought Paula, and was glad when Sergeant Cox opened the door and asked if they could help trace Mavis Bell's next of kin.

"She hasn't any," said Rupert shortly.

"She must have somebody. A friend, maybe."

Rupert insisted that there was no one.

"Then who deals with her affairs?"

"Her lawyer. The guy who killed her."

"Then perhaps you could tell me the name of the firm."

Eventually they left Rupert resigning himself to further

questioning, and came out into the chilly early morning hours.

Heathview Villas looked very peaceful, the outlines of the big Victorian mansions showing plainly against the London night sky. For a moment or two they all three stood by the gate of Bertram Revelson's house.

"I wonder if he's considered famous enough for them to put a plaque on the wall saying he lived here," remarked Carol.

"And Mavis Bell died here," murmured Paula. "Right now she's more famous than he is."

"Even more so when the news breaks," said James. "Murder-writer murdered. Carol—" James turned to the girl—"why did you say 'Gordon Vincent of course' when we asked you who you'd been chasing? You didn't say 'of course' to the police."

"Didn't I? I can't remember what I said. Oh, I'm so tired." Carol gave an enormous yawn. "I can't stand up a moment longer. See you tomorrow. But it is tomorrow now. Thanks for everything."

They watched her walk quickly towards the house next door.

"That was odd," said James. "That wasn't like Carol."

Paula, disappointed in her wish to give Carol the letter, turned in the other direction. "I'm past all thought," she said. Then suddenly she stopped: "James—was that one of ours?"

A small cat had suddenly appeared in the lamplight, and it shot across the road into the darkness beyond.

"Hope not," said James. "Let's hurry up and see."

They found the kittens sleeping peacefully, and in the shortest possible time they were doing likewise.

Morning brought a strong sense of anticlimax, a great rush to get on with the day's business, and a feeling that last night's events had never taken place at all, that it had all been a dream.

It was not until the late afternoon that Paula found an

opportunity to speak to Carol alone. James had run into Dr. George Montague, who had been visiting one of the houses in the Villas, and they had gone off to a pub together for a drink and a chat. It would be an hour at least before he returned.

Carol was on her own, watching a television panel game. The living-room felt peaceful and it was not even particularly untidy. "Don't tell James," said Paula as she handed over the letter. "He's in a very law-abiding mood at the moment."

"It's Mum's handwriting," said Carol, opening out the pages. "Oh Paula, how can I thank you? I'm not going to read it. Shall I burn it, or shall I give it to her?"

"I'd give it to her," said Paula, "but it's up to you."

"I think you're right. She's much better, but Dr. Garrett said she should stay in bed for a day or two. On the whole the police have been quite considerate."

"And how is Melissa?"

"She's fine. Very fed up at missing all the excitement last night."

"Is she home too?"

"She's having a bath."

"Melissa is always having a bath," said Paula. "Carol, I know you're sick of talking about it, as we all are, but if you want to thank me, you can tell me why you said 'Gordon Vincent of course' last night."

"Of course I will," said Carol, looking slightly embarrassed. "I didn't mean to be rude to James, but I was so tired, and the thought of explaining—"

"Yes, I know," murmured Paula, and then she added more briskly: "Gordon. I thought you wanted your mother to switch to his law firm."

"Yes," admitted Carol, "but that was before I found out that he'd been stealing his clients' money. Rich and helpless old women."

"When did you learn this?"

"A few days ago. Rupert told me."

"Rupert?" Paula was surprised. "I didn't know you were friendly with him."

Carol smiled. "If you really want to keep something quiet, you can, even in Heathview Villas."

"Rupert," said Paula again. "Did Chris Williams know?"

"Not even Chris," replied Carol. "Rupert's very discreet."

"He sure is that." Paula was still feeling somewhat disconcerted. "And he doesn't gossip for the sake of it. I suppose Chris knew about Gordon, though."

"Of course. We couldn't think what evidence Chris could have got hold of, but of course Gordon couldn't risk anything being found there after Chris died."

"So he came back to try to find out what there was, and found Mavis there first. Oh, no." Paula interrupted herself. "Mavis couldn't have forced the lock. She must have followed him in and interrupted the search."

"Yes, that's what we thought," said Carol simply.

"You've told the police, of course. What I don't understand," added Paula, "is who sent that warning note to Gordon."

Carol looked puzzled. "What warning note?"

Paula explained her theory about the letter that Sylvie had seen Gordon pick up from the doormat.

"Maybe it was something quite different," said Carol. "An invitation or something. He didn't need any warning notes to know it was time to disappear."

Paula was still not satisfied, but time was passing and she wanted to be home before James returned. "Carol," she said, standing up, "may I tell James that you and Rupert—"

She found it difficult to finish the sentence. James was going to feel rather hurt. He had befriended Carol, he had befriended Rupert; he liked them both, and he would be bound to feel that they had not been quite open with him. And yet one could understand it so well. James and I hate to think that everybody in the Villas knows all our business, said Paula to herself.

Carol was looking even more embarrassed. "There's

nothing much to tell," she said. "We just like to meet without having the feeling that the whole road is discussing us."

"I know," said Paula softly. Then she added, "There's no need to make a drama of it. Let it come out naturally sometime or other."

"Thanks. That's Mother calling. I must go."

Half an hour later James returned home, bringing with him the Montague doctors, George and Sheila, and a large carrier bag.

"Since we never got round to our dinner party," he said to Paula, "we've decided to share a Chinese takeaway. I hope that's all right with you."

Paula was delighted: Congenial company was what they both needed, but after they had eaten she learnt that there was a particular reason for the visit.

"It's all yours, George," said James.

"Mavis Bell was a patient of mine," said George Montague. "Sheila used to look after Mrs. Potts, who most certainly killed herself, by the way. She was deeply depressed. I gather that there have been rumours—anyway, no more of that now. Mavis Bell."

He paused for so long that his wife had to nudge him.

"Mavis left a confession," he said abruptly. "It's on tape. Her secretary had instructions to give it to me in the event of her death. It was originally intended to be given to her solicitors, but in view of the present situation in that firm—"

"Could you make it a bit more snappy, dear," said Dr. Sheila Montague. "Paula and James have been very patient up till now."

"Sorry," said George. "I'm afraid your patience is going to be needed for a little longer. Ours too, because we don't know what's on the tape. Mrs. Leaming is bringing it to me tomorrow. She has only worked for Mavis for a short while, by the way. Mavis sacked her regular secretary last week."

"I know," said Paula. "Annie told me. Poor Annie. She'll never get that book finished now."

"She'll have material for a better one if she chooses to write it," said George, "except that she's not invited to the party."

"What party?" This was James.

"Mrs. Leaming said Mavis wanted a selected group of people to hear her confession. Sheila and me. You two, Rupert Barstow, Jill Race and daughters; Chris Williams and Bertie Revelson, both no longer available, and Gordon Vincent, also not available for different reasons."

"Have you told the others?" asked Paula.

"No. You're the first. The question is, where do we hold this gathering?"

Sheila suggested that it should be held at Jill's, but her husband disagreed. "They've had trouble enough, that household," he said. "It must be in the Villas, but it would be best on neutral ground, and not where any big drama has taken place."

"I think that means us," said James to Paula.

"That's fine by me," she said. "When is this to be?"

"Tomorrow evening?"

"Yes. Anything in particular required—cassette-player?"

"Mrs. Leaming will see to everything," promised George.

24

"Shall we have the kittens in?" asked Paula the following evening as they were shifting chairs around the big room.

"I'd like it," replied James, "but I've a feeling they could detract from the solemnity of the occasion. This is Mavis's show, and I believe she didn't like cats."

"Cats in the kitchen, then," said Paula. "I'm feeling dreadfully nervous. Do you think we are in for one of those explanatory speeches at the end of the classic detective story with the least likely person being pointed out as the murderer?"

"Mavis is dead, and it seems more than likely that it was Gordon who killed her. We're only listening to a tape," James reminded her.

"I know, but I'm still nervous. I find the whole business rather creepy. I'm sure she is going to accuse somebody."

"If it's Gordon, the police are after him in any case. There's the bell."

Ten minutes later the whole company was assembled, with the exception of Melissa.

"She's too young," said her mother, "and I don't think she's fit for it. Neither am I, for that matter, but since you all made such a point of my being here—"

Several people got up to fuss over Jill, to rearrange her footstool, and bring her another cushion.

She's getting better, thought Paula; she's much more like her old self again.

"When you are all ready," said Mrs. Leaming, who was sitting on an upright chair beside the table on which stood the cassette-player.

Paula recognised her as the silhouette she had seen in the window of Mavis's office. A tallish, youngish woman in a businesslike dark suit and with very well cut dark hair.

There was silence in the room, then came the faint click of the recorder, and then Mavis's voice, quite clear, but sounding older and weaker than she had in person.

"I want to explain and to ask you to forgive me. Not that that matters because I'll be dead when you listen to this. But still—"

Here the voice tailed away into a short coughing fit. It sounded even older than before when it resumed.

"I've had a very boring life. Boring because I never really cared for anybody or anything. Oh, of course I've had love affairs and I even had a child once. I didn't like him much and he didn't like me and I've no idea what became of him."

In the slight pause that followed this statement Paula glanced across at Rupert. He was looking distressed, and for one moment she thought, his mother deserted him, is it possible? But a hasty recollection of Rupert's age, not yet thirty, and of Mavis at over ninety, told her that it was not possible.

"Nor do I know where any of my relatives are," continued the voice from the machine. "I find personal relationships dreadfully tedious. I always have done. People make such fools of themselves with their little loves and jealousies and hopes and despairs. It makes good material for stories, that is all. And it's writing stories that has always kept me going.

"That's enough of myself. I am bored and I am boring, but I pretend an interest in people that I don't feel because one has to have some contact with them. But I have lived too long. Why should I, who have no interest in life, be given all these extra years, while others, who long to live, are not—"

Again there was a coughing fit and a pause. Paula looked around the circle of faces. Rupert still looked unhappy; Jill looked incredulous; Carol was sitting with her head turned and her long fair hair was falling over her face. The two doctors appeared very relaxed, and James, when Paula's eyes eventually came to rest on him, smiled at her briefly and reassuringly.

She smiled back. Mavis's voice continued.

"I've enjoyed writing my books, trivial as they are. It's given me money, which is the only thing that really matters, and it's also given me a brief flicker of interest now and then, an easing of the boredom. But a year or two ago my own inventive powers began to fail and I became very much afraid that I had 'written myself out,' as people do. What could be done? I needed a stimulus to the imagination and I could find none in the lives that were going on around me. Of course I could have started travelling again, as I have done before when such sterility of fantasy threatened, but the very thought of it was so tedious that I soon put that idea aside.

"And then the answer came. If the lives around me were producing nothing of interest, why didn't I do something to stir them up? What makes people act? Money, ambition, love, curiosity, and fear. A guilty conscience. That's a great stimulus. Get people's consciences working and you get something happening.

"Anonymous letters. It came to me in a flash. I knew plenty about the residents of Heathview Villas, and it wasn't difficult to find out more. For my own purposes it didn't matter if it was rumour or truth. All I wanted was to observe the behaviour of the recipients. I started with Gordon Vincent. Are you listening, Gordon? There were only some general hints about your professional untrustworthiness. You're a tough nut, Gordon. There was no reaction to my letter at the time, but as I am speaking now, it looks as if matters could soon come to a head. Perhaps they will already have done so when this tape is played.

"Then came Jill Race. Easy prey. Presumably she is listening to me speaking now, so I won't go into detail of what I think of her personally. Unfortunately I did not get much opportunity to observe the results of that letter. The next one was Bertie Revelson, who almost immediately got himself killed in rather unusual circumstances. That startled me, I must admit. In fact it upset me. I didn't actually want people to die, nor even to suffer much, but just to *do* something. Of course the possibility of a suicide is always present in the case of poison-pen letters, but I had hoped, by including in the letters a great deal of religious nonsense, that the recipients would not take them all that seriously. I wanted them to feel guilty and anxious and threatened, but not to the point of taking their own lives.

"Bertie worried me. It was almost certainly an accident, but still . . . That is when I began to suspect that somebody had got wise to what I was doing. More of that in a moment. Let me crow over my chief success. Paula Glenning, a most intelligent lady of some literary reputation. From what I could gather, I got her really alarmed and I also thoroughly aroused her curiosity. That was most gratifying. I wrote a few more letters. Annie Lawrence reacted very satisfactorily, and since I had the pleasure of watching her reactions at close quarters while we were cooperating on a book, I have not put her down as one of those who should be invited to listen to this tape.

"Two people I had decided from the first that I would not include. One was my neighbour, Martha Potts. She could do nothing to suprise or interest me. Why should I disturb her nostalgic dream of an existence? But she died. She killed herself, I believe, as I should probably have done before now had I not been inspired to produce some interest in my life, some reason for continuing to exist. I was very distressed by Martha's death. I felt somehow responsible for it."

The voice on the tape wavered, and there was a considerable pause. Paula looked around the room. All the faces were very serious now. They were like children listening to a story, not a happy or cheerful story, but an unpleasantly gripping one. Her own part in it had been brief and not as bad as it might have been. What about the others? Who was to come next?

"The other person I left off my list," continued the voice on the tape, "was Rupert Barstow. There was plenty I could have said about him, but he was too near to me, and I was too dependent on him. I needed Rupert's help to move my word processor in and out of my office, to drive me to the Clinic where I receive some help for the arthritis, and where I posted the letters. It is amazing to me that nobody, as far as I know, has yet noticed the times and places that the letters were posted. Elementary detective work would have tracked down the writer, but you all seem to have been so preoccupied with the content of the letters and your own reactions to them that such rational deduction appears to have been ignored."

"That's not quite true," said Paula in the slight pause that followed this statement.

Mrs. Leaming switched off the tape and turned to George Montague.

"Does anybody else want to make any comment?" he asked. "Or shall we listen to the end before we discuss it, if indeed we want to discuss it at all. There's not much more."

"I agree with Paula," said James. "Some of us have been thinking about the mechanics of the letter-writing and posting, but I think we'll say no more until we have listened right through."

"I don't see how we could have compared the letters," protested Jill, "since we didn't know who had received them."

"And whose fault was that?" demanded Carol, suddenly sitting upright and glaring across the room at her mother.

"Let's not have any post mortems," said Rupert sharply. "Let's disappoint the ghost of Mavis."

Carol subsided, and George Montague nodded to Mrs. Leaming to start the tape again.

"It was very amusing to start with," said the voice of Mavis, "but when the deaths began I got frightened. And when Chris Williams found out that I'd been sending the letters, that was the end of all pleasure in my experiment. I don't know how he did it except that he has a genius for unearthing things about people that they don't want anybody else to know. Are you listening now, Chris? Or has somebody rumbled you and stopped your little game forever?"

At this point there was a stifled scream from Jill, and Carol jumped up and ran across to her mother's chair, and sat on the arm and held her mother's hand tightly.

Mavis's voice went relentlessly on.

"Chris and I have a lot in common. Secret power. Or rather, his pleasure is in power, mine is in curiosity. When Martha Potts died and Chris told me he knew I'd been writing the letters, it all turned into a nightmare. It was his game now, not mine. You didn't want money from me, did you, Chris? You wanted revenge on Rupert because he wouldn't play with you. You wanted everybody to believe that Rupert had poisoned Martha Potts so that he could inherit her money. I knew he hadn't but I had to play your game, Chris, because there was something you knew, something I really cared about, and . . ."

Mavis's voice, which had been getting more and more agitated, faded away into a fit of coughing. Paula looked around the room. Tension was mounting. Even the two doctors were looking less relaxed than they had before. James was leaning forward in his chair, Rupert's expressive face was grimmer than ever, and Carol seemed to be having difficulty in controlling her mother's agitation.

Mavis's coughing fit ended and her voice came through again, clear and steady.

"You are an evil man, Chris Williams. One day one of your victims will kill you. Perhaps they already have."

"Stop it! Turn it off!"

It was a loud cry from Jill. She pushed Carol away, struggled to her feet, screamed again as the injured ankle took her weight, and began to stagger towards the table on which the cassette-player stood.

Carol and Rupert ran to support her, everybody began to speak at once, and Mrs. Leaming switched off the machine.

"I'm taking my mother home at once," said Carol angrily when Jill had calmed down a little. "If I'd known it was going to be like this I'd never have let her come."

Sheila Montague, standing by Jill's chair with a hand on her wrist, said soothingly, "We're very sorry about this. Please believe me, Carol, George and I had not the slightest idea what was on that tape. We hadn't even seen it, let alone played it. Mavis left it with Mrs. Leaming, with instructions that she should contact George to arrange this meeting."

Carol was only slightly mollified. "As if my mother hadn't been through enough already—"

"If you're going, I'll come with you," said Rupert, moving up to Carol. "I don't want to hear any more either."

"Just a moment, please."

It was Mrs. Leaming's voice, quiet and controlled as before, but with a new note in it, a note of authority. Everybody turned to look at her, with varying degrees of surprise. Even Jill paused in her muttered complaining and stared, with mouth slightly open, at the tall woman in the dark suit.

"There is a little more on the tape," she continued, "but since it is of no concern to any of those present, I shall not play it now." She was extracting the tape as she spoke and putting it into her handbag. "If anybody particularly wants to hear it, perhaps they will get in touch with me tomorrow morning through the employment agency. After that it will not be available."

She snapped her purse shut and looked as if she was about to depart.

"Excuse me," began George Montague, "but as one of the executors of Mavis Bell's will—"

"You may be an executor," said Mrs. Leaming, "but I have the greater right to this recording."

"You were employed by Mavis Bell at the time of her death," said George Montague, "but I hardly think—"

"I have evidence here," interrupted Mrs. Leaming, opening her handbag again, "if anybody insists upon seeing it. Copies of the birth certificates of myself and my father. Mavis Bell was my grandmother."

There was a stunned silence.

"My father, being illegitimate," continued Mrs. Leaming, "bore his mother's name. John Bell. He died a few months ago. My mother and I—I am an only child—have always wished to make contact with Mavis out of a certain curiosity—perhaps a morbid curiosity—to try to discover what sort of woman could treat my father so neglectfully. He was the kindest and best of men." For a brief moment the steady voice seemed to falter slightly, and then it went on: "We would do nothing while my father was alive. He didn't wish it, but we had our plan. I earn my living as an agency typist, and my mother is an assistant librarian. It wasn't difficult to find out where Mavis lived and to place myself on the lists of the employment agency she used, but we certainly did not expect to become involved at such a dramatic moment in her life, nor in her death."

Mrs. Leaming, who had sat down again while she was talking, now came to her feet once more. "There's not much more to say. Our original intention was certainly not mercenary, but since my mother and I are by no means rich, and since we have discovered that Mavis, unlike her neighbour, took the precaution of protecting her assets from theft by criminal solicitors, we have decided to claim our inheritance. I am Mavis Bell's rightful heir. That is all."

She took a few steps towards the door, then paused: "I

have carried out Mavis's wishes, and tomorrow afternoon I am going to hand this tape over to the police. They have not yet tracked down Gordon Vincent and I most sincerely hope that they never will. If it ever happens that he is arrested and accused of causing Mavis's death, then I shall come forward myself and confess to the killing. She was a wicked woman. I understand her better now, but I cannot forgive her. Goodnight."

The door closed behind her. Jill was the first to speak. "Get me home, Carol," she murmured. "I'm feeling quite sick."

Rupert got up to help, and the three of them made their slow way out of the room.

"I really ought to apologise," said George Montague after they had gone, "but truly I hadn't the least idea what we were going to hear, and when Mrs. Leaming asked me to help her carry out Mavis's wishes—"

"There's nothing to apologise for," said James. "It's all over, and personally I'm going to try to forget it."

"Me too," said Sheila Montague. "We'll leave you folks in peace now and get in touch later."

James accompanied them to the front door. When he returned to the big living-room he found Paula curled up on the sofa with her head buried in a cushion. "I'm sorry," she muttered. "I can understand how Jill feels. That was nasty." She rubbed a hand across her eyes and sat up. "Where are the kittens?"

"I'll let them out of the kitchen."

"And please may I have some of your China tea?"

Ten minutes later Paula had recovered enough to sip her tea and throw a little paper ball for Sally to chase.

"I know you don't want to talk about it, James," she said, "but I can't help wondering. When Mrs. Leaming said that if Gordon was arrested she would confess to killing Mavis herself, did she mean she'd really done it? What do you think?"

James groaned, picked up Sam, held him up for a moment

with all four paws dangling, and addressed him sternly: "It's no good, my lad, we're not going to have any peace. She's got another mystery to worry at and we're never going to hear the last of it."